TJ tipped up her head until her eyes met his.

"We will get to the bottom of this. I promise. And I'll be right here to help you as long as you want me."

He realized his last words could be taken more than one way.

Alexis must have heard it too. He watched an unmistakable desire flare in her eyes.

Slowly, Alexis placed a soft hand over his chest. Their gazes locked on each other.

She glided her hand over his chest and up to his shoulders, leaning in.

TJ's heated gaze searched hers before falling to her mouth.

Then he grasped her wrists gently and eased her back. "I'm sorry. I can't do this."

Confusion mixed with the lust in her eyes. "Why not?"

Why not? It was a good question, one he suspected she wouldn't like his answer for.

"I'm supposed to be protecting you."

SILENCED WITNESS

K.D. RICHARDS

Harlequin
INTRIGUE

To Allison Lyons, an amazing editor. Thank you for believing in me and making me a better writer.

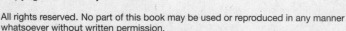

Harlequin® INTRIGUE™

ISBN-13: 978-1-335-59169-2

Silenced Witness

Copyright © 2024 by Kia Dennis

For questions and comments about the quality of this book, please contact us at CustomerService@Harlequin.com.

TM and ® are trademarks of Harlequin Enterprises ULC.

Harlequin Enterprises ULC
22 Adelaide St. West, 41st Floor
Toronto, Ontario M5H 4E3, Canada
www.Harlequin.com

Printed in Lithuania

Recycling programs for this product may not exist in your area.

MIX
Paper | Supporting responsible forestry
FSC® C021394

K.D. Richards is a native of the Washington, DC, area, who now lives outside Toronto with her husband and two sons. You can find her at kdrichardsbooks.com.

Books by K.D. Richards

Harlequin Intrigue

West Investigations

Visit the Author Profile page at Harlequin.com.

CAST OF CHARACTERS

Thaddeus Jeramiah "TJ" Roman—Private investigator for West Investigations and Mark's former best friend.

Alexis Douglas—Private chef and sister of Mark Douglas, who is accused of espionage and theft.

Mark Douglas—Alexis's brother, who is suspected of theft and espionage.

Nelson Bacon—CEO of TalCon, a government contractor that makes cyber weapons.

Arnold Forrick—Nelson Bacon's right-hand man at TalCon.

Jessica Castaldo—Mark's on-again, off-again girlfriend.

Chapter One

Alexis Douglas awoke with a start and listened. She'd heard something, or she thought she had, but all was still in her darkened bedroom and there was no sound in the house. She closed her eyes and settled deeper into her soft mattress.

She was on the cusp of falling asleep when she heard the sound again.

Her eyes flew open.

A thin beam of light snaked through the blinds on her bedroom window. Her neighbor's security lights. Maybe Ronnie was out on his back porch. He liked to have a cigarette from time to time and his wife wouldn't allow him to smoke inside their home.

Alexis focused, listening again for the sound that had awakened her. She heard nothing. But she couldn't shake the feeling that something was off.

A minute ticked by. Then another, with each moment increasing the apprehension twisting her stomach into knots.

Creeaak.

She knew that sound. It was a loose floorboard, one of many in the sixty-year-old house she'd bought a year ago with the intention of fixing it up. She'd been too busy with her business as a personal chef to do any renovations other than to the kitchen, which had become her favorite spot in the house.

Alexis bolted out of bed, crouching down in the narrow space between the wall and the bed frame. Her eyes darted over the darkened room for a weapon or a way out. The bedroom was on the second floor, so jumping from the window was a last resort. Unfortunately for her, she liked to keep her space clean and the clutter minimal. No random cutlery sitting around from a midnight snack. Her clothes were hung, by color and season, in her closet or folded neatly in the dresser. The only thing on her nightstand was the hardback she was slowly making her way through. She'd even left her cell phone downstairs to charge rather than plugging it in next to the bed, which was supposed to be the healthier choice according to an article she'd read earlier that week.

Now, she was looking at facing an intruder with nothing but the latest Naomi Hirahara thriller to defend herself with.

But she couldn't just stay cowering next to the bed. She'd be cornered if the intruder came into the bedroom. Same with hiding in the closet.

Another floorboard creaked down the hall.

She grabbed the book from her bedside table, and as quickly and quietly as she could, hurried toward the bedroom door. Flattening her back against the sliver of space between the doorframe and the dresser, she listened for sounds of the intruder entering the room.

Time felt as if it were moving in slow motion. Sweat beaded on her skin, making it sticky even though she'd turned the thermostat down to sixty-six before she'd gone to bed.

The faintest sound of rustling material came from the hall, followed by the soft fall of footsteps.

Trembling, she held the book against her chest as the bedroom door slid open slowly.

Her chest tightened even as it seemed to her as though every breath rumbled into her lungs with the force of a locomotive.

The intruder, a man based on the build, in dark-colored pants and shirt, crept toward the bed. She wasn't a small woman, five-seven with ample curves and she worked out regularly, but she could see that the man had several inches and at least thirty pounds on her. And although it didn't look like he had a weapon on him, there was no way for her to be sure of that. Still, she had to do what she could to protect herself.

She didn't move until the man's back was fully to her. Then, lifting the book high above her head, she raced forward with a battle cry she hoped would catch him off guard.

He turned, his eyes wide in the eyelet cutouts of the ski mask he wore over his face.

She slammed the book into his jaw with all her strength, then let it fall to the floor as she turned and ran. Three-hundred-fifty pages might stun, but it wouldn't incapacitate a man of his size. She had to get out of the house fast.

Her bare feet slapped against the wood floor of the hallway. She made it to the top of the stairs before a hand grabbed her roughly from behind and she was thrown to the floor. She landed on her back and the intruder was on her before she could make any attempt to get to her feet.

His hand clamped down over her mouth, muffling the scream that tore out of her throat. She bucked and thrashed, trying to throw him off or free an arm or leg to lash out with, but she'd been right about his size being no match for her.

Tears leaked from her eyes as he leaned in close. He smelled of whiskey, tobacco and something else. Something foul and more than a little threatening.

Fear ricocheted through her body.

The man smiled maliciously, and she knew that he was getting off on terrorizing her. Was that what he was there for? To terrorize her? Assault her? Worse?

Her heart thudded so hard it felt like it was only seconds away from beating right out of her chest.

The man pressed himself against her, and her entire body shuddered.

His smile grew wider, sending her fear spiking. He brought his face within centimeters of hers. "Stop asking questions about your brother or you'll end up just like him."

He lifted his hand from her mouth, but her scream was cut off by his fist connecting with the side of her temple.

She was only vaguely aware of his weight lifting off her before she was plunged into darkness.

Chapter Two

Sitting at his desk at West Security and Investigations in the late afternoon, Thaddeus Jeremiah Roman—TJ to everyone except his mother—put the finishing touches on his report to the wife of a wealthy Manhattan hedge fund manager who suspected her husband of cheating. Mrs. Hedge Fund Manager had good instincts. She was dead on with her suspicions about her husband cheating, but she'd suspected the wrong woman. Her husband wasn't seeing the twenty-something female associate he worked with but his secretary.

TJ had a feeling Mr. Hedge Fund Manager was about to find out the true meaning of cheaters never prosper. Mrs. Hedge Fund Manager had explained in no uncertain terms when she'd contracted with West Investigations for their services just what she would do to her husband's nether regions if they found evidence he was cheating. And that was before she took him for everything the courts would allow.

And that was reason number 1,582,392 why TJ was never, ever getting married. Not that he'd ever cheat on his nonexistent wife or any other woman he was seeing. He was always up front with the women he dated. He didn't want a serious relationship, and he wasn't looking to have his mind changed at this point. The only woman he'd ever loved had died right as they were on the cusp of building a life together. He hadn't been sure he was going to make it through the loss. And he wasn't interested in feeling pain like that ever again. No, it was better to keep his relationships nice and easy. Surface level. If a woman couldn't deal with that, he wished her well and went on his merry way.

TJ filed his report and sent it off to his boss and co-owner of West Security and Investigations, Shawn West.

West Security and Investigations was one of the best private investigations and personal security firms on the East Coast, and with the recently announced Los Angeles office, the firm was poised to expand its reach nationwide. They'd investigated and gotten to the bottom of cases that included everything from corporate espionage to organized crime. They also provided personal security for some of the wealthiest and most recognizable people in the world, most recently Brianna Baker, one of the hottest actresses in Hollywood at the moment. Most of the investigators who worked for West Security and Investigations preferred to take on the sexier, high-profile assignments, but not TJ. If it was between a case that was likely to see him dodging bullets or a good old-fashioned adultery investigation, he'd take the adultery, please and thank you. A decade in the Army had been more than enough excitement to last him a lifetime.

Now he just wanted to collect a steady paycheck, cheer on the Nets, and make a pretty woman smile from time to time. A simple life.

The sound of the door to the office opening and heels clicking over the tiled floors caught his attention. It was after five. Serena Wells, their receptionist, had already left, and most West employees didn't keep regular hours, coming and going as needed. He was the only West employee currently occupying a desk in the open floor plan office space.

He peeked over the top of the partition surrounding his desk.

A woman with dark micro braids cut into a swingy bob framing her face swept into the office. The first thing he noticed was her curves. She had them for days, and she apparently knew how to make the most of them. Dark blue jeans stretched over a round behind and a bronze V-neck sweater clung to an ample bosom. She marched to the reception desk wearing brown leather boots that matched her sweater, with a black wool coat thrown over her arm. Smooth, dark caramel skin that looked like it had never seen a blemish covered her heart-shaped face.

Even from several feet away, though, he could read the tension in her body. She paused at the empty reception desk, her eyes glazing over the space.

Her gaze landed on him before he could fall back behind the safety of the partition. He didn't like engaging with the clients any more than he had to. Generally, he interacted with them just enough to get the information he needed to do the job and to convey his results. But for some inexplicable reason, he found himself rising and moving toward the woman before he fully comprehended that was what he was doing.

The woman's brown eyes bore into him as he drew closer to her. There was something about her. Something familiar.

"TJ? TJ Roman?" Her gaze shifted over him from head to toe and back in open assessment.

The sound of his name from her lips gave him pause. He knew that voice. Alexis? It couldn't be and yet it was.

Surprise sent his brow into an arch. "Alexis Douglas?"

She smiled crookedly. "I didn't know if you'd remember me."

"Of course." He started toward her, his arms outstretched to give her a hug. It was awkward.

Alexis was the sister of his best friend. Well, he guessed former best friend now. He hadn't spoken to Mark Douglas in over two years, although the loss of the friendship that had begun in grade school still stung. It had been even longer since he'd seen Alexis. More than ten years had passed. She was barely legal back then, a fresh-faced eighteen-year-old heart-stopper. But now... He stepped back, letting his gaze roam over her. She'd grown up to be flat-out gorgeous.

Alexis was four years younger than her brother Mark, which made her five years younger than TJ. The distance in their ages and the fact that she was the sister of his best friend had meant he'd barely noticed her as they'd grown up. But he was noticing her now. The attraction he felt for the woman standing in front of him was instant and strong. Strong enough that he had to remind himself that she was still his friend's sister and still off-limits. That was good for another reason. Based on the anxiety he saw in her dark brown eyes, Alexis hadn't sought him out for old times' sake.

"What are you doing here, Alexis?"

She licked her plump lips nervously. "I need your help."

It took him an extra second to process what she said, given the amount of blood that had moved from his brain to his groin while he'd been looking at her lips.

"Let's go into the conference room and you can tell me about it." He finally managed to get out.

He led her into the conference room, offering her coffee or water, both of which she declined before taking a seat. She sank into the black leather chairs at the long conference table, moving her purse from her shoulder to her lap.

There were plugs in the center of the table for laptops and tablets, and he knew a lot of his colleagues liked taking digital notes, but he preferred pen and paper when he had the choice. He grabbed one of the yellow legal pads stacked on the table and a pen.

"Okay," he said, "start from the beginning."

Alexis took a shaky breath and let it out slowly. "I guess it began with Mark's death."

Chapter Three

Alexis gave TJ a minute to process what she'd just said. She hadn't been sure if he'd heard about Mark passing. She knew that her brother and TJ had had some sort of falling out a couple of years earlier, but Mark would never talk about exactly what happened. Mark had always seen her as his little sister. Someone he had to protect, no matter how old she'd gotten. That protection had extended to bullies, boys, and any information that he thought she didn't need to trouble her pretty little head with. But Mark was gone now and he couldn't protect her from whoever had broken into her house two nights earlier.

"Mark is dead?" TJ cocked his head to one side, saying the words as if he was trying them on for size. Like they didn't fit.

Because they didn't. It had been two months, and she was still trying to process living in a world without her brother in it.

She pushed back the tears threatening to spill from her eyes. "I didn't know if you knew. Or if you wanted to know. I'm sorry to spring it on you like this." This was harder than she'd imagined, but she didn't know who else to turn to.

"How?" TJ's voice came out as little more than a whisper.

"Officially? Suicide." She gripped the strap of her purse

so tightly now that her knuckles whitened. But she didn't think Mark had committed suicide, a belief she suspected was at the root of her current troubles.

TJ's eyes went hard. "No way. No. Way."

Buoyed by his categorical rejection of her brother's official cause of death, she slid closer to TJ. "Mark died two months ago. Before he died, he was under suspicion for several crimes."

"What kind of crimes?"

"I'm not sure exactly. All I could get out of him was that there had been a theft of some sort at the company where he worked and he'd been suspended pending an investigation."

TJ frowned. "I don't believe Mark would steal from anyone."

Hearing his conviction that her brother was innocent felt like a thousand pounds had been lifted off her shoulders. She leaned toward TJ, sitting in the chair next to her. "Me either. Mark wouldn't tell me much about it. You know how he was about protecting me from anything and everything even remotely unpleasant."

TJ gave a small smile. "I do remember he was a bit overprotective of you, yes."

"More than a bit," she grumbled. "He hadn't been arrested or anything, but I know he'd hired a lawyer."

"So it was serious." TJ rubbed his chin with the hand not holding the pen.

"Very." She nodded. "And that seems to be the basis for why the authorities believe that Mark committed suicide. He was found in the apartment he rented. It looked like he swallowed a bottle of Valium." She caught a sob before it bubbled out.

For the first two weeks after she was notified of her

brother's death, she hadn't stopped crying. She didn't know if she would be able to stop if she let herself start again. Mark needed her to be strong now. To prove he hadn't committed the crimes he'd been suspected of and that he hadn't killed himself.

TJ gave her a moment to collect herself before asking, "Where did Mark work?"

"TalCon Cyber Security. The company is a major government contractor headquartered in Virginia. Most of the work they do is for the US military."

"I've heard of it," TJ said with a frown.

"Mark did something with computers for them similar to what he did when he was in the Army. I don't really understand what he did, but I know my brother. Mark was an honorable man. He wouldn't have done anything to disgrace himself, and he wouldn't have killed himself. He intended to prove his innocence."

"That sounds like Mark."

Alexis sucked in another deep breath. The conversation with TJ was going well, but if it was going to go off the rails, it would be with what she said next. "TJ, I think Mark was murdered."

He said nothing for a long moment.

"Alexis—"

"Listen, I know what you're going to say. I've already heard it from the cops handling Mark's supposed suicide. And his lawyer. But I know…" her voice caught, "knew my brother. I'm hoping that because you knew him too, you'll help me."

TJ shrank back in his seat away from her.

Damn him, he wasn't going to help her.

"I don't know what I can do to help you," TJ started. "I

chase after cheating husbands and people who are trying to defraud their insurance company."

"You work for one of the best private investigations firms in the city," she said incredulously.

"I chase after *very rich* cheating husbands and wives," he repeated with emphasis. "I don't investigate theft and potential murder."

"You could," she said, hating the desperation in her tone. But she needed help, and she was willing to do whatever it took to get it. "I looked into this firm, and this should be a walk in the park for West Investigations. Didn't your boss bring down an organized crime syndicate in the city last year?"

"I am not Ryan West," TJ grumbled.

This had been a waste of her time. He wasn't going to help her.

Alexis threw her shoulders back and stood. "Fine. I want to talk to him then."

TJ remained seated. "Sit down, Alexis."

She sat, the fire suddenly going out of her. She was so tired. Tired of the grief. Tired of the not knowing. She needed to move on, but to do that she had to know the truth, and to get that, she needed help.

"If I'm crazy, if I'm just a grieving sister looking to excuse her brother's bad decisions, why did someone attack me in my home two nights ago?"

She had his full attention now.

TJ leaned forward in his seat. "Attack you? What are you talking about?"

"Two nights ago, someone broke into my house and attacked me." Her voice caught again, thinking about the man's weight pinning her to the floor. "He threatened me, then knocked me out so he could get away."

She'd done what she could to cover the bruise on her face with foundation and had styled her hair to fall over it. She pushed her braids aside now. The makeup helped but couldn't hide the injury completely.

Something akin to a growl rumbled from TJ as he inspected her face.

She let her hair fall back over the mark.

"What kind of a threat?" he barked.

"The man said if I didn't stop asking questions, I'd end up just like Mark."

TJ's expression turned even darker and, although she knew it wasn't aimed at her, deadly.

"Did you call the police?"

She nodded. "I did. They took a report, but I don't think much will come of it. The lock on my front door had scratches, like it had been jimmied, but nothing was taken and I couldn't give the officers a description of the man who attacked me. He wore a mask."

"Give me a description. In fact, walk me through that night. Every detail you can remember."

She did as he asked, pushing aside the fear that ripped through her anew as she recounted the man throwing her to the hallway floor and climbing on top of her.

"Did he…" TJ shook with rage, unable to complete his sentence, but she knew what he was asking.

She shook her head again. "No, thank God."

The man hadn't been there to hurt her, not in any serious way, at least. She knew that now. His objective had been to terrorize her, and he'd succeeded.

She finished telling TJ about that night, watching his

jaw flex in anger as she did. She knew she shouldn't, but she found it sexy. TJ had always been a handsome man. She put him at six two or three, taller than Mark had been at six feet, but they'd both developed the lean, hard bodies of soldiers. It looked like TJ kept up his physique. Powerful biceps filled out his pullover. He still kept his hair in the short cut favored by the military, but the hard line of his square jaw was dusted with stubble.

She remembered Mark catching her admiring TJ on the sly one time when they'd both been home on leave. He'd forbid her from dating TJ, which had led to an argument. He didn't have any right to tell her who she could and couldn't date. After all, she had been eighteen at the time, a grown woman and fully capable of deciding who to date.

It hadn't mattered, anyway. TJ hadn't so much as looked twice at her on the several occasions they'd met previously. Mark had made a point of making sure she knew that TJ was a player who never kept a woman around for long.

She'd glimpsed his naked left ring finger now. Unmarried. It didn't seem like much had changed over the years for him. It was just as well. Her last relationship had ended disastrously, and she wasn't sure when, or if, she'd even be ready to jump back into the dating pool.

"Look, I'm not going to give up on clearing Mark's name. If you won't help me, I'll go to Ryan West. And if West Investigations won't help me, I'll keep looking until I find someone who will."

TJ sighed. "Are you sure about this? I mean, someone has already broken into your house. I know Mark wouldn't want you to put yourself in any danger. Maybe the best thing to do is to let the cops handle this."

She leaned forward and looked him in his eyes. "I'm

more sure than I've been about anything else in my life. Mark protected me when he was alive. It's my turn to protect him the only way I can now."

TJ looked away from her, staring out of the conference room window for so long she was sure he was coming up with a gentle way to tell her to get lost.

She was nearly ready to tell him to forget the whole thing and go find another private investigator when he turned back to her.

"Okay, I'm in."

Chapter Four

TJ looked up at the sound of a knock and spotted Shawn West on the other side of the glass door.

"I need to step into the hall for a moment," he said to Alexis before getting up, leaving her to review West's standard contract on her own.

"I hear you've bought in a new client," Shawn said, craning his neck to see inside the conference room.

TJ stepped into Shawn's line of sight, blocking his view of Alexis. "Something like that. She's the sister of a friend."

Shawn stepped back and gave him a searching look. "I see. And what does this sister of a friend want us to help her with today?"

"Her brother may or may not have committed suicide after being accused of stealing from his employer. It looks like her questions have drawn some unwanted attention."

Shawn co-owned West Security and Investigations with his brother Ryan. Ultimately, it was up to the two of them which cases West Investigations took and which they passed up, although they gave their investigators a lot of latitude.

TJ gave Shawn a quick rundown of everything that Alexis had told him, including the break-in at her home and the attack on her.

Shawn whistled sharply. "That sounds like a more complex case than the ones you normally take on. Are you sure you're up for it?"

No, he wasn't sure at all. But he was sure that he couldn't just palm Alexis off on another West operative.

"I can handle it," TJ growled.

Shawn gave him a knowing smile. "Why is it that all our cases lately seem to revolve around beautiful women in trouble who tie our male employees up in knots? What's going on around here?"

TJ cocked his head to the side. "Isn't that how you met your wife?"

Shawn chuckled. "Touché. I know you are used to being a lone wolf and all, but let me know if you need any help."

A lone wolf. The idea sparked a moment of sadness in him before he pushed it away. "Will do. I'll probably need to make a trip to Virginia. It's where Mark, my friend and Alexis's brother, lived and worked."

"When are you thinking about leaving?"

"Tomorrow, if that works for Alexis. I don't want to leave her alone, though, so I will take you up on that offer of help and ask that you assign someone to stick with her until I'm sure she's not in any danger."

"No way." Alexis's voice boomed behind him.

He turned, annoyed with himself for being oblivious to the sound of the conference room door opening.

Alexis squared off with him, her hands on her hips. "I'm going to be right by your side for any and all investigating."

TJ sighed. "Alexis—"

"Nope." She held her hand up in a stop motion. "I don't want to hear it. Mark is my brother. I'm the client, so it's my rules or I go to another private investigations firm."

TJ looked to Shawn for help but quickly assessed he'd be getting none from his boss.

Shawn shrugged. "She is the client, and it wouldn't be the first time we let a client tag along."

TJ cast his eyes to the heavens, hoping for some divine help, although none appeared forthcoming.

"Fine," he growled, remembering something Mark had once told him about his sister. She could be incredibly bossy. And she almost always got her way. TJ recalled thinking that was because she had Mark wrapped around her little finger, but now he wondered whether that was it at all. Alexis Douglas was a force.

"I was just saying to Shawn that our first stop should be Virginia."

She nodded. "That's fine with me. The police finally released his apartment and his landlord has given me until the end of the month to move Mark's stuff out so we should have no problem with access."

Since she seemed to be in a somewhat agreeable mood, TJ pressed on. "And, in light of the attack at your place, I am going to suggest you have a bodyguard tonight and any time I'm not with you."

She nodded again. "You won't get any argument from me. That creep getting into my home was terrifying." A small shudder worked its way through her body.

The urge to pull her into his arms and assure her he wouldn't allow anything to hurt her hit him.

"Great," he said and instead of acting on his impulse, he turned to Shawn. "Is Tess or one of the other female operatives available?"

"I'd prefer it if you took the job," Alexis spoke up. "That is, if it's okay with you."

He turned back to her. "It's okay with me. I just assumed you'd be more comfortable with a woman staying with you overnight."

Alexis gave a lopsided smile. "I think we'll manage." Sobering quickly, she added. "Mark trusted you and so do I."

The air between them charged. He wasn't sure if she was right about Mark trusting him, but it made him unexpectedly happy to hear that she did.

"It does make things simpler since you will be headed to Virginia tomorrow," said Shawn, breaking the tension smoldering between TJ and Alexis.

TJ dragged his gaze from Alexis's face with Herculean effort, but he still couldn't seem to get words to form, so he simply nodded his acquiescence to the plan.

"Good. Now that that's all settled," Shawn said, with a clap of his hands and a salute before sidling away toward his office.

"Now that that's all settled…" TJ mimicked his boss. He wasn't sure, but he thought he heard Shawn chuckle before he disappeared around the corner at the end of the hall. "I have a go bag in my car, so I just need to grab my laptop from my desk and I can follow you back to your place."

"Yeah, sure. Great. I'm parked in the garage right next to this building."

"Come on." He stepped to the side of the hall to let her pass in front of him. "Let's go find out what happened to Mark."

ALEXIS PULLED INTO the driveway of her small two story. She waited until TJ pulled in behind her and opened the driver's side door before she got out of her car. Ronnie, her next-door neighbor, sat on his front porch in a puffy orange vest and a pair of shorts, even though it was mid-October and the temperature hovered just above fifty degrees outside. Ronnie was what her mother used to call "a character" but, with the exception of his penchant to talk far too long about anime, he was harmless.

She threw a wave to Ronnie, then moved to the front door quickly in an effort to avoid being pulled into an endless conversation.

TJ threw his duffel bag over his shoulder and met her on the porch. "Your neighbor seems awfully interested in your comings and goings." He glared at Ronnie. "Or do you so rarely bring a man home that we're causing a neighborhood spectacle?"

Alexis opened the door and stepped inside her home before answering him. "I've never brought a man home before."

A quick flash of surprise swept across TJ's face before he smiled. "I'm honored to be the first."

Alexis pulled her gaze away from his, ignoring the pluck of awareness she felt when he smiled at her. A smile that made his already handsome face even more so.

He stood close. Her foyer wasn't large, and between the two of them, there was a mere sliver of space. She yearned to close it. He was big and strong and she knew he had training she couldn't conceive of. Ever since the break-in, she hadn't felt comfortable in her own home, but now, with TJ here, she finally felt safe.

And maybe a little something else too, but she wasn't sure she wanted to explore those feelings. Not so soon after Lamar. Well, soon might be a stretch. It had been a year since she'd walked in on her then fiancé in their bed with another woman. She and Lamar had been heading for a breakup for months, riding the downward wave of the relationship neither one of them had the courage to officially end. Coming home to their shared apartment and finding him with another woman hadn't hurt nearly as much as it should have, but her self-confidence and her belief in her ability to judge people had taken a significant hit.

She cleared her throat and looked away from TJ's penetrating gaze. "So, let me show you around the place." She did a sidestep and hurried farther into the house. "There isn't much to it. This is my office." She pointed to the room to the right. "It's supposed to be a formal living room, but what do I need with a formal living room?" She could feel herself babbling, but couldn't seem to rein it in. "Back here is the kitchen, dining nook and informal living space. I guess the family room, but of course it's just me. No family."

A shard of grief knifed her when she realized how true that was. Her mother died when she was nineteen, and she and Mark had never known the father who walked out on his family when Alexis was still an infant. Now, with Mark gone, she was well and truly alone. But it wasn't the time to wallow in that thought.

"Um, the two bedrooms are upstairs. We'll have to share a bathroom, but I don't think that should be a problem. It will be like we're back in college." She laughed awkwardly. "Or I guess the military for you."

Shut up!

Her brain seemed to have finally hit the switch that shut off her mouth.

"Your place is nice," TJ said after a moment. He sat his duffel bag on one of the kitchen chairs.

"Thanks. I know it needs some work. I bought the place last year with the intention of doing it all, but you know how life is." She shrugged and let out another nervous chuckle.

TJ's mouth quirked upward in a sexy half smile. "I know how life is."

She moved farther into the kitchen. "The one room, of course, I had to renovate, even before I moved in, was the kitchen." She swept her hand out as if she was a showgirl introducing the headlining act.

For a chef, the kitchen was kind of like a stage. And she'd wanted to make sure her kitchen had everything she could ever dream of. Or at least everything she could afford to dream of at this stage in her career.

TJ did a three-sixty turn, taking in the entire space. "It's stunning. I remember how you liked to cook when we were growing up."

"I've turned it into a career," she said, moving behind the large center island. "I'm a personal chef. I have several private clients in Manhattan and Brooklyn. A couple in Connecticut and Westchester." She hesitated for a moment before blurting, "A friend of mine has even invited me to partner with her to start our own restaurant. I'd be the executive chef."

TJ's smile grew. "Wow. I'm impressed, but not surprised. I'm sure you're a fantastic cook and you'll have people flocking to your restaurant."

A warmness flooded her insides at his praise. "You should probably reserve judgment until you've eaten something I've cooked. Sit. I'll get started on dinner."

He moved his bag to the floor and sat. "You don't have to cook for me. We can order something in."

She pressed a hand to her heart. "You wound me, really you do. Just sit there and keep me company."

His laughter filled the space. "You're the boss. In the kitchen, that is."

Now she laughed as she got to work making penne all'arrabbiata, which was a spicy pasta that was an uncomplicated yet tasty dish she was used to making for several of her regular clients.

While she cooked, TJ worked on his laptop.

After a silence that was far too comfortable, she plated pasta and carried both plates to the table.

"It smells amazing." TJ closed the laptop and set it aside.

She slid into the chair across from him. She'd pointed him to the wine rack in the corner of the kitchen while she'd been cooking and had had him open a bottle of red. She'd had a glass and a half while she'd cooked and TJ topped off her glass now.

"You don't drink?"

"Not when I'm on the job. Just water for me." He tapped the rim of the water glass next to his plate.

"That's too bad," she said, reaching for her glass. "This is a really good year."

TJ smiled. "After this job is over, we can share a bottle."

A smile slid over her lips and she realized she actually liked the idea of going out on a date with him.

The meal was starting to feel too much like a date. She sipped her wine and reminded herself that getting involved with TJ was a horrible idea. He'd been a ladies' man when they were young, and men like that didn't change. Not to mention the very fact that she was attracted to him was enough reason not to pursue anything. Her judgment in men was atrocious, hence her self-imposed hiatus from dating.

She needed TJ's help to prove Mark's innocence, and that was all she needed him for.

"This doesn't just smell good, it tastes out of this world. Wow! You are an amazing chef." TJ said, forking another bite into his mouth.

She felt herself preening under his praise. The dish showcased her cooking style perfectly. She was all about flavor and taste. Of course, there was something to be said for creating dishes that looked appetizing too, but what people really remembered, and what kept her clients coming back for her services, was tasty comfort food.

"I remember you cooking all the time with your mother. She was an amazing cook, too. Is that why you became a chef?" TJ asked.

She circled the rim of her glass with her index finger. "In part, I guess. I think I associate cooking with taking care of people. I know my mother did. I don't know if I have the maternal gene like she did, but I have a talent in the kitchen and good food makes people feel good. If I can put more good in the world, that makes me happy."

TJ swallowed another bite and reached for his glass of water. "Why do you think you don't have the maternal gene?"

"Oh." She waved a hand in front of her face. She wasn't sure why that comment had slipped out. Too much wine maybe. "I don't know."

"You've never been married?" TJ pressed.

"Never married. I got close, kind of, a year ago." Now she knew she'd had too much to drink. She hadn't meant to open that door, but now that she had, the look on TJ's face made it clear he wasn't going to let her drop it without getting the whole story.

She sighed and took another sip, fortifying herself. "It's pretty much a cliché at this point. I came home early one day and found my fiancé in bed with another woman."

"You're better off without him."

"That's what Mark said." She knocked back the remaining wine in her glass. "But you didn't even know Lamar."

TJ shook his head. "Don't need to. He's a moron and you deserve better."

"Thank you."

A frisson of electricity passed between them.

After a long moment, TJ spoke again. "So currently, no serious boyfriend?"

"No serious boyfriend. No boyfriend at all." Her voice snapped with tension.

"Why not?"

"I don't know," she said, avoiding his gaze now. "I guess I'm just not ready to jump back into the dating pool yet."

She rose and carried her still half full plate to the sink. She hadn't finished her pasta, but she'd lost her appetite. Hopefully, she'd eaten enough to soak up some of the wine that had loosened her lips. "I'm exhausted. I'm going to go to bed. Leave the dishes. I'll clean up in the morning."

TJ rose, bringing his empty plate to the sink. "You cooked. I'll do the dishes. And I'm sorry if I made you uncomfortable."

She tried for a smile, but it felt tight across her face. "Don't worry about it. You don't know uncomfortable until you've been a woman working in a five-star restaurant kitchen." She stepped around him and headed for the stairs.

"Alexis," TJ called out.

She turned.

He looked at her for a long moment, as if he wanted to

tell her something. Then the moment passed. "I booked us on a seven o'clock flight to Dulles. I hope that's not too early."

"Not too early at all. I'll be ready."

"Goodnight, Alexis."

"Goodnight, TJ."

Chapter Five

Alexis went to her room after dinner with every intention of finally getting some rest. She hadn't had a good night's sleep since the break-in and attack. That plan was sidelined by a phone call from her best friend, Karen Hall, known to her friends as Kitty.

"So, how did it go?" the ever-vociferous Kitty asked without preamble.

Kitty knew about the break-in at Alexis's house and her plan to enlist TJ's help to investigate Mark's death and the accusations of theft against him.

"TJ's on board," Alexis said, settling in under her duvet. Calls with Kitty tended to run long. "Actually, he's here now. He's staying in my guestroom tonight, and tomorrow we're headed to Virginia."

"Wow, that was fast. I tried looking him up online, but I couldn't find anything on a Thaddeus Roman. Zero social media presence, and there's no staff directory on the West Investigations website."

Alexis chuckled. "Well, there wouldn't be. He's a private investigator. Emphasis on the private. Wouldn't exactly be private if he had a ton of photos of himself floating around on the net."

"I guess," Kitty said sulkily. "Okay, then tell me about him."

It occurred to Alexis that TJ and Kitty might be just each other's types. Kitty shied away from serious romantic relationships, just like TJ, preferring to "cast her net wide," as she liked to say.

"Hello? Alexis, are you still there?"

Kitty's voice pulled her out of her reverie. "Yes, I'm here. Sorry, spaced out for a moment. What do you want to know?"

"What does he look like? Paint a picture."

"I don't know. I guess he's handsome. He's about six foot two, broad shoulders. I think I remember Mark mentioning he played football in high school and he looks like it. He can be kind of surly, but he's got these light brown eyes with flecks of yellow in them and sometimes when he looks at me there's such gentleness in them."

"Flecks of yellow, huh? Sounds like you've been staring into Mr. Roman's eyes quite a bit," Kitty teased.

"It's not like that," Alexis said quickly. "It's just something I noticed."

Kitty laughed. "Okay, if you say so. You know it's okay to have feelings for a man," she added soberly.

Kitty had been there for her through the breakup with Lamar. She'd been gently nudging Alexis to get back into the dating game for a while.

"I know."

"Have you thought any more about my offer?"

Alexis had met Kitty in culinary school, but while Kitty was an adequate chef, she really flourished at restaurant management and finance. Her financial acumen was most likely a result of being the daughter of a prominent investment banker, but whatever the cause, Kitty's knowledge of food, finance and marketing had made the restaurants she currently owned two of the most popular dining spots in Jersey City at the moment. Kitty was currently in the process of opening a third restaurant, this one in Manhattan's Financial District and pressuring Alexis to sign on as partner and executive chef.

"I'm still thinking." When Kitty sighed, Alexis added, "It's a big deal. I'd have to let go of my current clients, give up the business I've already built in order to take on a restaurant."

"I know, I know. I told you to take all the time you need, and I meant it, but it would be so great to run a restaurant together."

She and Kitty spoke for a half hour longer about the restaurant and what they'd do together if Alexis agreed to sign on before hanging up.

Talking to Kitty usually invigorated Alexis, but tonight thinking about what her future could be only made her think about Mark and the future he'd never have. More than just having his future cut short, his name would be forever sullied if she wasn't able to prove that he wasn't a thief who'd committed suicide rather than face the consequences of his actions. She couldn't let that stand.

After receiving the call that Mark had killed himself, she'd made the trip to his home in Virginia. Mark rented one side of a duplex apartment, but she hadn't had the strength to clear out his stuff then. Mark's landlord had offered to do the job, but just the idea that all that was left of her brother could be placed into boxes and shipped to her had kept her from taking him up on his offer.

Maybe she'd be strong enough to go through a few of

his things on this trip. Take the things she wanted to keep for herself and bring everything else to the Salvation Army or donate them to local families in need. Mark would have liked that.

She plumped her pillow and willed her mind to shut down so she could get some sleep, but two hours after she'd gotten into bed, she was still wide awake.

It wasn't just that she'd be going to Virginia tomorrow and, hopefully, getting some answers about her brother's death. Every time it felt like sleep was on the horizon, her mind drifted to TJ in the room across the hall and her brain perked right up again, as well as other parts of her body.

No matter how many times she told herself she should keep things on a friendly level with her brother's former best friend, she couldn't keep her mind from entertaining other ideas. Every time she looked into his perceptive brown eyes, she felt as if he could read her mind. Not a good thing, given the activities that were in her head when she looked at him.

She hadn't been attracted to a man since Lamar. But based on what Mark told her about his friend, TJ might be the perfect man to test the waters again with. After all, his no-strings-attached approach to relationships meant neither of them would end up hurt when it inevitably ended between them.

But finding answers about Mark's death was the most important thing she had to do at the moment. Getting involved with TJ now might jeopardize that. She needed him. It had been no accident, her seeking him out. While his friendship with Mark had seemed to wither, the neighborhood grapevine hadn't. She knew that he'd left the military and gotten his private investigator's license. From there, all it took was an internet search to find him. It was her good luck that he worked at one of the best investigation firms in the city. And because of her very wealthy clientele, she could afford to pay top dollar. At least for a while. She hoped that TJ's status as a military veteran would help open doors and loosen lips she hadn't been able to open or loosen on her own.

She rolled over onto her back and looked at the ceiling. "This isn't going to work." But she desperately needed to sleep if she was going to be any more help than a walking zombie tomorrow.

She got out of bed and slipped on her robe. A mug of warm milk always helped her to relax enough to fall asleep.

She opened the door to her bedroom and came face-to-face with TJ. He stood in the doorway of his room in his jeans and sock feet, but bare chested.

"Are you okay?" he asked.

She struggled to pull her gaze away from the curls of hair on his hard chest. But when she did, she found herself even more enthralled by his face. The shadow of stubble that had lingered on his face during the day was thicker now, propelling him from merely handsome to ruggedly sexy. The urge to jump him and have her way with him right there in her hallway was nearly overwhelming.

After much too long a pause, she finally got her brain to circumvent the lustful thoughts and form words. "Fine. Just couldn't sleep."

She turned away from him and moved toward the stairs. Space. That's what she needed right now. A whole lot of space between her and TJ Roman.

Unfortunately, it didn't look like she'd be getting it. TJ followed her down the stairs and to the kitchen.

She circled the large island, putting it between herself and TJ, and reached inside the refrigerator for the milk. "I'm making myself a cup of warm milk. Would you like some?"

"Sure."

"Why are you still up?" she asked as she got started on the milk.

"I was doing some research on Mark and the theft he was suspected of."

She set the pot of milk on the stove and turned the burner on before turning to face him. "Did you find anything?"

TJ shook his head. "Not much, but that's not surprising. If the charges hadn't yet been placed against him when he died, his name isn't likely to appear on public sources."

Alexis put the milk back in the fridge and closed the door with more force than was necessary. "I can't believe anyone would even think Mark could do what they are accusing him of."

She grabbed two mugs out of the overhead cabinet. A companionable silence fell over the kitchen in the couple of minutes it took for the milk to warm. She wasn't used to having another person in her space and was happy to find that TJ didn't feel the need to fill every moment with chatter.

"Can you take me through everything you know about the case against Mark? Everything Mark told you and everything you found out on your own?" TJ asked.

She poured milk into the two mugs. "I've already told you everything I know, which sadly isn't a lot, but I'll happily tell you again if it helps."

She slid one of the mugs across the counter to him, then turned off the burner and settled onto the stool next to TJ.

"You served with Mark in the military."

TJ nodded.

"I don't know much about it, but he was involved in cyber security. He got out of the Army a few years before you did and joined TalCon doing basically what he'd done for the Army, from what I understand."

TJ nodded again. "TalCon is a major military contractor. They employ hundreds of ex-military personnel, so that makes sense."

"Basically, Mark worked his way up until he was head of TalCon's cybersecurity unit. Several weeks ago, an important program Mark had been working on was stolen. Mark wouldn't tell me all the details, but he was accused of the theft. TalCon suspended him."

"It must have been a pretty important program," TJ mused. "Is that when he got a lawyer?"

Alexis nodded. "Yes, I think so. He hired Sanjay Atwal."

"But Mark wasn't charged with the theft right away?"

"No, but I know the police were putting a lot of pressure on Mark. I could tell he was under a lot of stress. He was worried."

"Sounds like he might have had reason to be."

Alexis frowned. "The Alexandria police department took the lead on the investigation into Mark's death, but I know they've spoken to the executives at TalCon. The detective on the case all but told me that she believes Mark killed himself because of the guilt he felt about stealing the program and because he didn't want to face the consequences of that." She pushed her now lukewarm cup of milk aside. "My brother was no coward, TJ."

He reached for her hand and gave it a squeeze. "I know he wasn't. I know firsthand how courageous your brother was. He saved my hide more than once when we were deployed."

Something shifted in his gaze.

"What happened between you and Mark? You used to be so close and then it seemed like almost overnight you guys grew apart."

Sadness swam across TJ's face. For a moment, she thought he might tell her, but then he fixed his face back into a neutral expression. "Let's stay on topic. Did the Alexandria police department give you any other information?"

She shook her head, resigned to the fact that she might never know what went down between her brother and his friend. "No. I know that they haven't officially closed the case because the medical examiner hasn't gotten the full toxicology screen back from the forensics lab. I've called Detective Elaine Chellel—she's the detective in charge of Mark's case—every week since getting the news of his death, hoping that the toxicology report will come in and prove Mark didn't take his own life, but so far nothing."

"Even when the tox report comes in, it may not disabuse the detective of her theory." TJ voiced her fear. "She may still close the case as a suicide."

"I know," Alexis said quietly. "And if she does, we may never know what happened to Mark."

Chapter Six

The next morning, they caught a seven o'clock flight out of LaGuardia and into Dulles airport just outside of Washington, DC. West Investigations had accounts with all the major rental car companies. With a few swipes on the app on his phone, TJ was able to rent a midsize sedan. He'd discussed his game plan for the investigation with Alexis on the plane. Their first stop would be to TalCon. TJ didn't hold out much hope that they'd get any straight answers from the company, but they had to at least try. Alexis had met Nelson Bacon, the CEO of TalCon, when she'd come to DC to claim Mark's body and organize his affairs. Bacon had given her his personal cell phone number then, and she'd called that morning to set up a meeting with him and Mark's direct supervisor, Arnold Forrick, at TalCon's offices. He was interested in what Mark's employer had to say about the situation.

TJ pulled up to the gates at TalCon's headquarters at ten minutes to ten that morning and gave his and Alexis's names.

The guard at the gate checked their IDs against his list, then gave them directions to the visitor's parking area before waving them through.

TalCon's headquarters was composed of three, three-story cube-like white buildings with windows too dark to see inside. They formed a U-shape around a large parking lot.

After another round of ID checking at the receptionist's desk in the lobby of the building, he and Alexis were allowed to take the elevator to the third floor. After a brief wait, Nelson Bacon's assistant, a young woman with sun-kissed blonde hair, led them down a long hall to a corner office.

Bacon rose from the chair behind a large black desk as they entered the office. In his sixties, with gray-brown hair and posture so straight, TJ would have pegged Bacon as a former military officer even if TJ hadn't used West Investigations resources to look into the backgrounds of Bacon and Forrick.

Bacon had been a decorated retired Army General who'd left the military for an undoubtedly lucrative position in the private sector with TalCon. He'd been with TalCon for the last twenty years, working his way up to the position of CEO. His second-in-command, Arnold Forrick, had a similar military background with several awards and commendations to his name as well.

"Miss Douglas. It's a pleasure to see you again." Bacon stretched a hand across his desk, which Alexis shook. Bacon turned to TJ. "And you must be Thaddeus Roman."

TJ shook Bacon's hand.

"Thank you for seeing us on such short notice, Mr. Bacon."

Bacon waved at the chairs in front of his desk. TJ and Alexis sat.

"As I said when we met some weeks ago, anything you need, we at TalCon are here for you, Alexis. I hope I can call you Alexis?"

"Yes, please do."

"What can we do for you today, Miss Douglas?" Arnold Forrick had stood stoically beside his boss's desk while they'd engaged in opening chitchat with a scowl that looked to have been etched onto his face.

Bacon's eyebrows arrowed down in a frown. "Please forgive Arnold's abruptness."

Alexis gave a weak smile. "Nothing to forgive. I'm sure you are both very busy, and we'll try not to take up too much of your time."

"So what can we do for you?" Bacon said, reclaiming his seat behind his desk.

"I've hired Mr. Roman to help me look into Mark's death. He's a private investigator," Alexis said.

Since neither had asked what he was doing there with Alexis, TJ had already surmised that they'd checked him out, and the lack of surprise from either man when Alexis pegged him as a private investigator convinced him he was right.

Now, though, Bacon did look surprised. "I'd been told that Mark took his own life."

Alexis gritted her teeth. "I don't believe that. It's a conclusion based largely on the premise that my brother stole from this company, which I know he wouldn't do."

"I don't know who you've been speaking to," Forrick started angrily, "but the details of the projects this company is involved in are confidential. If you share any proprietary information, TalCon will take any and all legal steps to—"

"Mr. Forrick," TJ interrupted, more than a bit irked himself. "Why don't you hear Alexis out before you start threatening legal action?"

Forrick began to speak again, but Bacon raised his hand, stopping him. "Arnold, let Miss Douglas speak, please."

Alexis glared at Forrick. "Mark was not a thief. Mark was a soldier, as were you, Mr. Bacon. You know how much the Army values honor, integrity and truth. Those values meant something to Mark in, and out of, the military."

"I knew Mark," Bacon said. "I would have never believed he was capable of any of this. I don't know what you have been able to turn up or what the police have shared with you, and I'm not at liberty to share information myself, but I will say the evidence is pretty damning."

"TalCon has been cooperating with law enforcement and will continue to do so," Forrick interjected. "If you know anything about what your brother may have done with the missing program or who he might have sold it to, I strongly suggest you share that information with the authorities."

"I assure you I have been questioned by the police," Alexis growled. "Thoroughly. Mark never told me about the missing program because it was confidential and he didn't take it."

TJ scooted forward in his chair. "You can't tell us about the program that went missing, but can you tell us more about why you are so sure Mark is the one who took it?"

"As I said, we can't reveal—"

Bacon held up his hand a second time. Forrick fell silent, but his scowl deepened.

"TalCon was alerted that there had been an unauthorized download of the program. The warning was supposed to alert in real time, but it was delayed several days because of a system failure. Arnold is right that I can't get into the exact nature of the breach, but we took the report seriously and immediately opened an audit."

"And the audit implicated Mark," TJ said.

Bacon gave a slight nod. "Unfortunately, our security cameras were down for maintenance on the night in question. But we employ some of the most advanced computer security available here at TalCon. Mark's computer, ID, and randomly generated fob code were used to access the system and download the program."

"Fob code?" Alexis prodded.

Bacon reached for a small gray square about the size of an eraser and held it out for her to see. "A key fob, or fob as we affectionately call it around here. It generates an eight-digit code that, along with an employee's ID, must be entered into the computer in order to gain access to our system. The code changes every three minutes and is unique to every employee."

TJ's heart sank. Bacon was right. The evidence against Mark did appear to be damning, but that wouldn't stop him from turning over every rock looking for an answer that didn't involve Mark being a thief. He didn't have to ask to know Alexis felt the same way.

"Can you give us some general information about your company? What kind of contracting do you do for the military, that sort of thing?"

"We can't—" Forrick started.

"You're a prominent weapons development company and a large government contractor," Alexis said. "We're not asking for any information we couldn't find on our own, but getting it from you now would be a help."

Forrick looked at Bacon, who stayed silent for a long

moment before nodding. He launched into a mostly use-
less recitation of the company's history.

"When did you realize that the software was missing
from your inventory?" TJ finally interrupted.

Bacon's expression tightened. "We were alerted by an
internal source."

"An internal source? What does that mean?" Alexis
pressed.

"I'm afraid we aren't at liberty to share that information," Forrick said. "And I'm afraid Mr. Bacon has to leave
now for his next meeting."

Bacon stood, underscoring Forrick's point. Meeting over.

It appeared they'd struck a chord, one TJ intended to
keep stroking until he got a sound he liked. Who brought
the theft to the company's attention?

TJ and Alexis stood and turned for the door.

"Oh," Alexis said, turning back to Bacon and Forrick.
"I'd hoped to speak with Mark's assistant, Lenora Kenda.
She had such kind words to say about Mark on the condo-
lence card she sent. I haven't had a chance to thank her."

The tightening in Bacon's jaw was so slight TJ could
almost convince himself it hadn't happened. Almost.

"I'm sorry, but Ms. Kenda is out of the office. She decided to take a few weeks off. She and Mark were close
coworkers. His death hit her hard."

Bacon's assistant was waiting for TJ and Alexis outside of the office. She stayed at their side until the elevator doors closed.

He and Alexis walked back to the rental car in silence,
but once they were safely inside the car and headed back
for the gate, Alexis spoke.

"That was a waste of time."

TJ shot a glance across the car. "You think?"

"You don't?" she shot back at him.

TJ chuckled. "Well, I learned that Bacon is hiding something. And that Forrick is his attack dog, so whatever it is Bacon is hiding, Forrick likely has a hand in it."

"You learned all of that from the little bit those two said up there?"

"It wasn't what they said, it was more what they didn't say and how they didn't say it."

Alexis's brow rose. "Okay. I'm going to have to trust your expertise on that."

"More importantly, they gave us a lead to follow." He navigated the car off of TalCon's campus and turned onto the road leading to the highway.

Alexis's eyes widened in surprise. "They did?"

"Lenora Kenda."

Alexis's expression took on a shade of skepticism. "Lenora? I only met her at Mark's memorial, but he talked about her a little over the years. It seemed like Mark trusted her."

It wouldn't be the first time Mark had trusted the wrong woman, but he kept that thought to himself. "I'm not saying she had anything to do with the theft or what happened to Mark. But I do find it curious that she's suddenly decided to take an extended vacation."

The skepticism remained on Alexis's face. "It could be just what Bacon said. She's just taking some time to process everything."

"It could be," TJ said, keeping his focus on the road ahead of him. "But I'd like to hear that from Ms. Kenda."

Chapter Seven

For now, Lenora Kenda would have to wait. Their second appointment of the day was with the attorney Mark had hired after being suspended from TalCon. TJ was hoping the lawyer could fill in some of the blanks Bacon and Forrick couldn't or wouldn't.

TJ allowed the voice on the GPS to direct him through the Alexandria streets. The lawyer's office was in the Old Town Alexandria area, and TJ could immediately see why it was called that. He drove down narrow, cobblestone-lined streets and passed quaint houses that had easily reached the century milestone and were still standing. Alexis sat in the passenger seat—her thoughts, though silent, filling the space in the car. Her frustration was palpable, but this was what investigations were like. Slow and steady, asking questions until someone gave you the answers you were looking for. Not nearly as sexy as they made it out to be in the movies.

TJ pulled the rental car to a stop in front of a two-story red brick house on a quiet, tree-lined street not far from King Street, Alexandria's main thoroughfare. A green sign with gold lettering stood in the front yard announcing, Law Office of Sanjay Atwal. Several of the other houses on the block had similar signs on the front lawns. Alexis had made an appointment for them. According to Alexis, who had spoken with him when she'd come to town to make Mark's final arrangement and several other times on the telephone thereafter, he appeared to be competent and to have had Mark's best interests at heart. She'd said that he'd seemed devastated when they'd spoken initially, which TJ hoped meant he'd be more helpful than Bacon and Forrick.

The receptionist greeted them, offering coffee, which he and Alexis declined, before leaving them to wait in what would have been a living room. Fifteen minutes later, the receptionist returned and led them into the back of the house, knocking briefly on a set of closed French doors, the glass shielded by closed blinds, before pushing the door open and showing them into Atwal's office.

"Alexis. It's so good to see you again." The man behind the desk stood, smiling, and took Alexis's hand in his, holding it longer than necessary. Atwal's gaze held a look that was unmistakable. The lawyer hoped to provide more than just legal services to Alexis. The realization sent an unexpected surge of jealousy through TJ.

Never gonna happen, buddy. The words surged through TJ's mind before he could remind himself that he had no claim over Alexis or who she chose to spend her time with. Still, until they got to the bottom of Mark's death and identified whoever had broken into Alexis's home, she was under his protection. And that meant no lecherous lawyers on his watch.

"Sanjay, thank you for seeing us on such short notice. This is TJ Roman. He and Mark were friends, and he's helping me sort out the events around my brother's death."

Atwal extended his hand toward TJ with a lot less enthusiasm than he'd had in greeting Alexis. "Mr. Roman.

Nice to meet you." Atwal looked him over slowly. When Atwal's gaze returned to TJ's face, he could immediately tell that the lawyer had sized him up as a potential rival for Alexis's affections.

Good.

No, not good. Not good at all, he admonished himself.

He and Alexis took seats in front of Atwal's desk. TJ studied the attorney while the receptionist made a second offer of coffee. He appeared to be in his mid- to late-thirties, dark brown hair just starting to show a bit of gray and light brown eyes that kept straying to Alexis's face. Mark had trusted the man enough to hire him, so despite the lawyer's obvious interest in Alexis, TJ tried to keep an open mind.

"So, Alexis, what can I do for you?" Atwal said once the receptionist closed the door, leaving the three of them in the room alone.

"I have some questions about Mark's…situation before his death. I'm hoping you can help me."

"I'll certainly do what I can."

"I don't think Mark stole anything and I don't think he killed himself," Alexis said.

Atwal sighed. "I had a feeling you were going to say something along those lines. I'd hoped you'd be able to let this go and move on with your life."

"I can't just let it go. I know Mark would never steal from anyone. And the idea that he'd take his own life? No. I know my brother. He wouldn't do what he's been accused of, and I can't let the world think that he did."

"Mark was never charged with a crime. His record was technically clean when he died."

"Technically, maybe, but we both know that TalCon, the police, and several others think he stole some sort of program from the company. And I can't even get anyone to tell me what kind of program went missing."

Atwal sighed again. "I can tell you that the program Mark is accused of having stolen is not just any computer program. It's more like a weapon."

A buzzing began in TJ's ears. "A cyber weapon."

Atwal nodded.

TJ was shocked but not surprised. TalCon held a number of known contracts with the US military, and who knew how many unknown contracts they had. Conventional forms of warfare were giving way to more technologically advanced weapons every day. And not just when it came to guns and rockets. The military recruited men and women who understood computers, programming, coding and all that computer jazz faster than the universities could graduate them.

"What kind of cyber weapon?" Alexis asked.

Atwal shook his head. "I don't know all the details. Some of it, I suspect, is highly confidential, possibly even classified. Mark was rather circumspect despite the pressure the company and the authorities were putting on him. TalCon had dubbed the program Nimbus. Technically, NimbusScriptPro. It's some sort of computer program that the company had hoped to sell to the military when it was operational."

"So the program wasn't actually being developed under a military contract," TJ said.

"No, which was good news for Mark," Atwal answered.

Alexis glanced between them with a confused expression on her face. "Why was that good news for Mark?"

Atwal folded his hands on top of his desk. "Because then the program would have technically been property of the US government and the consequences for Mark would have been far more serious than what he was looking at."

Alexis frowned. "I'd say the consequences were extremely serious as my brother is dead."

Atwal's expression softened. "I'm sorry if I sound callous. It wasn't my intent. Of course, the consequences of the accusations were very serious. I just meant that the matter was being treated as stolen private property rather than stolen government property. While TalCon is anxious to get the program back, they are also mindful of the damage to their reputation and stock price that couldn't be sustained if it becomes widely known that they've lost a significant piece of technology. It could have major effects on their current and future government contracts."

"So TalCon would like to get its property back and to keep this whole episode as quiet as possible?" That fit with the brush-off he and Alexis had received from Bacon and Forrick. With Mark dead, he was the perfect scapegoat if they could just find the stolen program.

"That's about the size of it," Atwal confirmed. "I planned to do my best to defend Mark if it came to that, but I have to tell you there was significant evidence that didn't weigh in his favor."

"We already know about Mark's ID card and fob being used to download the program, but those could have been stolen from him, right?" Alexis asked, sounding hopeful.

Atwal shook his head. "Mark didn't think so." He gave Alexis a sad look. "He was adamant his ID and fob were never out of his possession. But there's more." Atwal flipped open the manila file folder on his desk. "TalCon was tipped off to the fact that the program had been stolen when someone in the company's cybersecurity unit discovered a posting for it on a black market website for these kinds of things."

"An online weapons auction?" TJ said.

"Weapons, drugs, pretty much anything illegal." Atwal's face twisted in disgust, and TJ didn't have to imagine what other things were being sold online.

"I'm sorry. I think you two have gotten ahead of me," Alexis said. "What auction?"

"He's referring to the dark web," TJ explained. "It's like an alternative internet where criminals of all stripes buy and sell contraband and other illegal items, often using cryptocurrency."

Alexis nodded, seemingly having caught up. "And the program that TalCon thinks Mark stole is on this website? Why can't their cyber computer people just track the posting back to whoever put it up there? Then they'd know that Mark isn't the person who stole the program."

"I wish it were that simple." Atwal shook his head again. "The dark web is anonymous. That's why it works so well for moving illegal stuff. TalCon has enlisted the best of the best to try to track the posting, but so far they haven't had any luck in determining who posted it or even where it was posted from."

TalCon may have enlisted the best of the best, but TJ was pretty sure he knew someone better. Tansy Carlson, West Investigations' computer whisperer, had done things with a computer no one had ever dreamed possible. If the person who'd offered that program up for auction could be traced, she'd find them.

TJ made a mental note to ask Shawn for Tansy's help and returned his focus to the conversation at hand.

"What made TalCon focus on Mark?" TJ asked, redirecting the conversation back to what the lawyer did know rather than what he didn't. Even though Atwal had said he couldn't tell them much, it appeared he knew quite a bit about the case, and TJ wanted to keep him sharing information.

"The computer logs from Mark's work laptop. They show someone made an unauthorized download of the complete program from Mark's computer a week before the posting went up on the dark web. That was the only download of the program since Mark completed the most recent upgrades, and it wasn't authorized."

"Forrick and Bacon mentioned that they were alerted to the download by an internal source," TJ said. "You have any idea who or what that source was?"

The attorney shrugged. "I don't, and I don't expect TalCon or the cops will divulge that information without a court order, and we don't have grounds to get one." "So an anonymous source. That's not hard evidence," Alexis scoffed.

How difficult would it be for someone at TalCon to have accessed the program using Mark's credentials, or how hard would it be to cover up an unauthorized download? TJ suspected those questions were beyond the scope of the attorney's knowledge, but West Investigations had resources the attorney didn't. He'd put the problem to Tansy as soon as he could. Hopefully, she'd make more headway than TalCon's techs had.

Atwal closed the file. "It was enough for TalCon to put Mark on leave. And for the police to question him and get search warrants for his home and personal devices."

"And did they find anything?" Alexis spat.

"No. No, they didn't," Atwal conceded.

TJ got the sense that they'd gotten just about all they could from the lawyer. "Mr. Atwal, I was hoping you could give us the names of a few people we could talk to who might have more insight into this situation. You must have spoken to someone in the course of your investigation."

Atwal frowned. "As I said, Mark hadn't been charged with a crime yet, so I hadn't really started my investigation. I'd really only spoken to him about the case. But Mark did mention his personal assistant as someone I'd want to speak to if the matter moved forward." Atwal opened the file again and flipped through several pages inside. "Ah, yes, Lenora Kenda."

It seemed that Ms. Kenda's name was on the tip of everyone's tongue. "One more question and we'll get out of your hair. Do you happen to have a copy of Mark's autopsy report?"

Alexis shifted uneasily in the chair beside him.

He knew that aspects of this investigation might be difficult for her to hear and deal with, but reviewing Mark's autopsy report was crucial to determining whether or not the medical examiner made the correct call in categorizing Mark's death as a suicide.

Atwal seemed surprised. "Why...no. As far as I know, there wasn't a reason to do so."

Alexis slid forward in her chair and pinned Atwal with a look. "I think there is a reason. Can you get the report?"

"I... Well, I guess so. As Mark's next of kin, you're entitled to it, and I do know the medical examiner. Professionally." Atwal added quickly. "In my capacity as a criminal defense lawyer, I've had to speak with her on several occasions."

"Do you think you could convince her to make a little time to speak with us?" TJ pressed.

Atwal frowned. "I don't know."

"Please, Sanjay." Alexis reached across the desk and grabbed the lawyer's hand. "I couldn't tell you how grateful I'd be. I have to be sure about what happened to Mark."

Atwal's chest puffed out, and he gave Alexis's hand a squeeze. "She's always very busy."

"We'll only take up a few minutes of her time," Alexis pressed.

Atwal sighed. "I'll see what I can do."

Chapter Eight

Alexis was cautiously optimistic as TJ put the car in gear and pulled away from the curb. They'd gotten more information from Sanjay than they had from TalCon, and he was going to try to help them get even more. It was a start.

"It's after one," TJ said, breaking her from her thoughts. "How about we stop for lunch?"

The mention of lunch sent a pang through her stomach, reminding her that she hadn't eaten since before boarding the early morning flight to Virginia. "Sounds good." She took her cell phone from her purse and pulled up nearby restaurants. "There's an Indian restaurant with good reviews not too far from here."

"I do love biryani."

Using the directions on her phone, Alexis directed TJ to the restaurant.

Soft rock played from the overhead speakers and the smell of curry, saffron, and chicken swirled inside the space when they walked in. The lunch crowd, if there had been one, appeared to have already cleared out, and the hostess seated them quickly. A waitress in the standard uniform of black pants and a white shirt slid a plate of naan onto the table and took their drink orders. She returned a minute later with their drinks, having given them just enough time to scan the well-apportioned menu and decide on their meals, biryani for TJ and korma for Alexis.

For several minutes after the waitress left to put in their orders, they sat without speaking. They seemed to have entered into some sort of silent agreement not to talk about Mark or the investigation into his death and the theft, which suited Alexis just fine at the moment.

Alexis reached for a piece of naan and studied TJ.

"What happened between you and Mark?"

TJ coughed, choking a little on the sip of Diet Coke he'd taken just before she'd asked the question.

She supposed it was a little out of left field, but she'd always wondered. She'd asked Mark once, and he'd brushed her off, saying that they'd just grown apart, but she'd never bought that excuse. TJ and Mark were as close as brothers, growing up certainly closer than she and Mark had been, a fact that had led to more than a little jealousy on her part when she was younger. They'd even gone into the military together and, although Mark hadn't re-enlisted like TJ, she knew they'd kept in touch after Mark moved on, so it wasn't the Army that had driven them apart.

TJ had regained his composure, but he still hadn't answered her question.

"Why weren't you two as close as you used to be when we were growing up?" Alexis pressed. "And don't tell me you just grew apart."

"You're awfully bossy." TJ frowned.

She shrugged and waited.

"What did Mark tell you about it?" TJ responded finally.

"Not much. He always avoided answering whenever I asked about you."

He leaned back in his chair and gave a small smile. "I guess we still had some things in common then."

"I'm not going to let you joke your way out of answering the question," she responded pointedly. "Come on. You were like brothers. Brothers don't just stop speaking to each other."

The door to the kitchen opened and their waitress pushed through with a tray full of plates. TJ wore a hopeful expression, probably as much due to the ability to get out of the current conversation as to hunger. But his expression fell away when the waitress headed for a table on the other side of the dining room.

Alexis reached across the table and covered his hand. "Please. I feel like there's so much Mark kept from me. I know he was trying to protect me, but now that he's gone, it feels like I didn't really know him."

TJ's features tightened and the muscle in his jaw worked as he thought. Finally, he let out a haggard sigh. "I don't know if you ever met Mark's girlfriend, Jessica Castaldo."

Alexis's stomach tightened, and not due to hunger. She'd met Jessica. Mark had brought her along on one of his rare trips to New Jersey to visit her. Alexis had found Jessica to be spoiled and entitled. From what she saw during that short weekend, Jessica seemed more interested in the things that Mark was willing to buy for her than she was in Mark.

Alexis had forced herself to keep quiet, though. Her brother was a habitual monogamist. He only dated one woman at a time, but the relationships didn't seem to have much staying power. Most rarely lasted a full year. She'd prayed Jessica wouldn't be any different and had put on a happy face while they'd been in town.

"We met. I can't tell you how happy I was when Mark broke things off with her."

"I had a job that took me to DC two years ago and on my way back to New York, I stopped in Virginia to have a drink and catch up with Mark. He brought Jessica along. We all had a few drinks and...you know Mark."

She did. "He didn't handle his liquor well." It was the one thing she and her brother were in constant conflict about.

"No, he didn't, and Jessica, well, she was coming on pretty strong that night. I didn't encourage it, but I could tell Mark was getting angry." TJ looked away. "I should have ended the night early, walked away and gone back to my hotel, but I was concerned about leaving the two of them given how much they'd drank. Anyway, one thing led to another and Mark and I exchanged words. Honestly, I think Jessica enjoyed it. I suspect she instigated it a bit. Two men fighting over her, at least that's how I'm sure she saw it. I was just trying to get Mark to calm down and see reason."

"But he wouldn't." It wasn't the first time Mark had gotten himself into trouble with his drinking. She'd had to lend him money several years ago to bail himself out of jail after he was arrested on a DUI charge. She'd been livid. He could have killed himself or someone else. Mark swore it would never happen again and, as far as she knew, it never had. Her brother was such a kind, loving, thoughtful person when he was sober, but when he drank, it was like he was a totally different person.

Alexis had tried to talk to him on more than one occasion about his drinking and the possibility of getting some help, but Mark didn't believe he needed help. Instead of risking pushing him further away, she'd dropped the issue each time.

"We got kicked out of the bar, but I was able to get Mark and Jessica into a cab. Mark called me a couple of days later after I was back in New York to apologize. By then I was pretty angry myself. I called him out for thinking I'd ever disrespect him by going after his girl, and I told him his drinking was out of control."

"Let me guess, that didn't go over well."

TJ's brows went up. "You tried to talk to him about it, too?"

"Several times, but what is it they say? You can lead a horse to water..." she said sadly. She let the rest of the sentiment hang in the air.

TJ exhaled heavily. "That was the last time we spoke. I can't tell you how many times I've thought about picking up the phone, but honestly, I was more hurt than angry at Mark for even suggesting I'd hit on his girlfriend."

Alexis reached across the table again, this time squeezing TJ's hand, hoping it provided some comfort. "Hey, when he was drinking, Mark wasn't himself, but he knew you would never do anything to hurt him."

The expression on TJ's face said he wasn't so sure.

She gave his hand another squeeze. "I know you would never do anything to hurt Mark. You loved him as much as I did, which is why I knew I could come to you for help clearing his name and finding out what really happened to him."

"You can come to me no matter what. I hope you know that."

A spark of electricity shot between them. TJ turned her hand over, tracing a line from her ring finger to her wrist. His face had softened and Alexis wondered what his finger would feel like pressed against the pulse thundering under her skin.

"Excuse me."

They pulled apart at the sound of the waitress's voice. She slid their food onto the table and hurried away.

Alexis watched TJ's face morph into a mask of neutrality. She mentally cursed the waitress. Whatever moment she and TJ were having before the woman's appearance was clearly over, and Alexis couldn't help feeling disappointed.

Her phone chimed in her purse.

She fished it out and read the message on the screen.

"Sanjay says the medical examiner can see us at 2:30 today."

TJ glanced at his watch.

"Great. Maybe she'll have more of the answers we need."

Chapter Nine

TJ drove to the modern glass and concrete building that housed the northern district headquarters of the Virginia medical examiner's office. He parked in the parking lot shared with the forensics lab next door and walked with Alexis into the lobby. After giving their names to the security guard at the front desk, they signed in, passed through the metal detectors, and followed the guard's directions to the third floor.

When they stepped off the elevator, they were greeted by a second reception area manned by a male employee with a shiny silver name tag on his shirt announcing his name was Robert.

"Oh, yes, Dr. Bullock said you'd be coming in this afternoon," Robert said when he and Alexis gave their names a second time. "I'll let the doctor know you're here."

Robert rose and headed down a short hallway. After a moment, he reappeared. "Follow me, please."

They followed him into an office cramped with bookshelves and file cabinets, but that boasted two large windows overlooking the front of the building. A wide desk sat in front of the window and a woman with her long dark hair in a braid that hung over her shoulder sat behind it.

"Dr. Bullock, your guests." Robert waved a hand in the

general direction of TJ and Alexis as if he was revealing a prize on a game show.

The medical examiner stood. Dr. Jane Bullock was in her late forties or early fifties, petite and fine boned, with pale blue eyes that shone with intelligence.

He and Alexis introduced themselves and shook hands with the medical examiner before settling into the visitor's chairs in front of her desk.

Dr. Bullock let them get settled before speaking. "Miss Douglas, let me start by saying how sorry I am for your loss."

"Thank you," Alexis said quietly.

"I understand from your attorney, Mr. Atwal, that you'd like to see the preliminary autopsy report on your brother. It includes the standard blood tests we run in-house, but in this case Detective Chellel has ordered a more extensive toxicology report from our forensics lab." The doctor shuffled through a stack of files on her desk before pulling one free. "Here it is. I had my assistant make a copy for you to take with you if you'd like. I caution, though, that I am still waiting on the full toxicology results to come in. We're still pretty backed up from Covid, and suspected suicides don't get priority." The doctor passed the entire folder across the desk to Alexis.

TJ leaned over so he could scan the pages along with Alexis. The kind of investigations he typically took on didn't require reading autopsy reports. He had no idea what he was looking at. From her expression, neither did Alexis.

"I'm sorry, Dr. Bullock, would you mind summarizing the report for us?"

"Of course."

TJ handed the report back to the doctor. She ran through

Mark's height and weight, deeming them normal before running through her assessment of his vital organs.

TJ glanced at Alexis. Her face had taken on a gray, almost deathlike pallor. The medical examiner didn't seem to notice.

"Doctor," TJ interrupted. "We just need to know if you found anything unusual in the autopsy."

Dr. Bullock frowned. "Mr. Douglas's liver was beginning to show signs of liver disease. And of course, I found several undigested Valium pills in his stomach. That was consistent with the empty prescription bottle the police found in Mr. Douglas's apartment."

"But there were no signs of chronic drug use, right?" TJ pressed.

The doctor sighed. "I know where you're going with this line of questioning, and I won't have a definitive answer for you until the toxicology results are back. But I will say everything I've seen so far points to a diazepam overdose. I will be able to make a more definitive determination about cause and manner of death once I have all the test results back."

Not many people knew the distinction between the cause of death and the manner of death, but it was important. The medical examiner could rely on her examination of the body and the battery of tests that were standard in an autopsy to tell her what the cause of death was, such as a heart attack, gunshot, or as the cops suspected in Mark's case, an overdose.

The manner of death, though, required her to examine the totality of the circumstances to make a determination. A gunshot wound, for instance, could be self-inflicted or inflicted by a third party. The former would lead to the manner of death being listed as a suicide, while the latter would be a homicide. The same held for an overdose.

While it was the cops' job to track down the source of pills that had been the cause of Mark's death, the medical examiner was likely to be more forthcoming with information than the cops, which was why he wasn't upset that he and Alexis were able to speak to Dr. Bullock before seeing Detective Chellel.

"That I can't tell you. I do know that the only fingerprints that were found on the bottle of pills were those of Mark Douglas," she said pointedly.

Alexis frowned. "If someone had the wherewithal to try to make it look like Mark killed himself, I'm sure they'd have the foresight to wear gloves or wipe their fingerprints from the murder weapon."

Dr. Bullock looked as if she was ready to argue the premise. They needed the doctor on their side and willing to continue to answer their questions, so challenging her findings directly wasn't the best idea.

"Dr. Bullock," TJ interrupted whatever the doctor might have been prepared to respond to Alexis. "Did the toxicity screen turn up any other unusual substances in Mark's system?"

Mark's wasn't the first autopsy he'd read, but he was no expert. There were people he could tap at West Investigations to help him make sense of all the technical mumbo jumbo in the report and he would, but Dr. Bullock was here now.

"I ran the usual blood screening test and, except for the Valium, nothing unusual turned up."

"But the standard blood screening is limited, right?" TJ pressed gently. "It doesn't look for the more exotic potential substances that could debilitate a person."

Irritation flashed across Dr. Bullock's face. "Of course,

blood screening is much more limited than the full toxicology, and we can't test for every possible substance anyway. If there was any hint that something like that had been administered to Mr. Douglas prior to his death, the protocol is for the police to notify me and I can order the requisite tests to confirm the existence of such a substance or rule its use out. The police, in this instance, made no such notification."

"Of course," TJ said, backing off. "We're not suggesting that anything is amiss."

A soft snort slipped from Alexis, but the medical examiner either didn't hear it or chose to ignore it.

TJ couldn't help but wonder what Sanjay Atwal had told the doctor about his and Alexis's interest in Mark's death. "We just want to make sure we understand the scope of your report."

Dr. Bullock's steely expression softened marginally. "That is prudent of you. But I assure you that everything was done according to policy." The doctor turned her gaze on Alexis. "I am very sorry for your loss. My findings are supported by the evidence. Your brother took his own life."

Chapter Ten

It was after three, which meant they were able to check into the hotel TJ had booked for them. Alexis considered Dr. Bullock's findings as TJ drove, her mood dark. She'd pulled up the medical examiner's bio on the state website, so she knew the doctor was experienced and well trained. Still, she must have missed something because, deep in her heart, Alexis knew her brother. No matter what, he wouldn't have given up on life or on her. There had to be an explanation that fit with the medical examiner's findings and also proved that Mark hadn't killed himself. The question was, how did she find it?

She glanced over at TJ. He hadn't said much since they'd left Dr. Bullock's office, and Alexis was beginning to wonder if he regretted agreeing to help her. So far, they'd run into nothing but flashing signs declaring Mark's guilt.

TJ had made a reservation at a boutique hotel on the outskirts of Alexandria. It was a two-story structure, on the older side, but recently renovated. The rooms each had a window next to the door that looked out onto a shared courtyard and an outdoor pool. TJ had reserved a corner room on the second floor, a roomy one-bedroom, one-bath suite.

"This is a sofa bed," TJ said, tossing his duffel bag onto

the wide sofa in the living area of the suite. "I'll sleep here and you can take the bedroom."

That didn't seem fair at all. She wasn't a delicate flower who couldn't handle a night on a sofa bed. "That doesn't sound comfortable. I'm happy to alternate. One night on the sofa, the next in the bed for each of us, for as long as we're in town."

TJ shook his head. "The last thing I want is to get too comfortable. That's how mistakes are made. Plus, I'd rather be out here where I can keep an eye on things."

She shuddered as the memory from the night of the break-in rolled through her mind. She'd pushed the terror from that night into the recesses of her mind, trying to focus on clearing Mark's name, but it came thundering back at the worst times, reminding her that this wasn't just about Mark. She was in danger as well.

She and TJ settled into the suite and spent the rest of the afternoon working on the case. TJ called into West headquarters and, together with Tansy Carlson, West Investigations' computer whiz, was able to find a phone number and address for Lenora Kenda, along with a bunch of background information on the woman. Lenora didn't answer the phone when they called, so they had to leave a message. Alexis reached out to Detective Chellel with no success. She was sure the detective was avoiding her calls on purpose. The detective had made no secret of the fact that she believed Alexis was a grieving sister unwilling to accept that her brother had committed a crime and taken his own life to avoid the consequences of that act as the law closed in.

TJ sent the copy of Mark's autopsy report that Dr. Bullock gave them to Shawn West, who had more experience with such reports, hoping he'd see something the doctor missed. She and TJ sat on the pullout sofa on a video call going over the autopsy report with Shawn. Unfortunately, he only confirmed what Dr. Bullock had told them. They'd have to wait for the toxicology report to come in before any definitive conclusions could be made.

"We've left a message for the detective in charge of the case asking to meet with her but haven't heard back yet." TJ said. "I know Mark was a heavy drinker, but his using Valium was new information to me and Alexis."

"With everything he had going on in his life, it's not too surprising," Shawn responded. "Valium is an anti-anxiety and stress medication."

"Are you saying you think the police and the medical examiner could be right? That Mark could have taken his own life?" Alexis said, anger vibrating in her tone.

Shawn frowned. "I'm just thinking through the information you've gotten so far. It's too soon to draw any conclusions."

There was that line again. It was too soon to draw conclusions. But Mark was dead, so it seemed to her like they were far, far too late.

She rose and walked to the window. She knew she didn't have a right to be angry at Shawn West. He was only restating the facts. But her attempt to prove Mark's innocence seemed to be doing just the opposite.

Frown lines appeared above Shawn's brow. "I can't say what the cops will find suspicious, but it's definitely a question worth asking when you do get a hold of the detective in charge of the case."

"Thanks, Shawn. I appreciate your help with this," TJ said, signaling an end to their conversation.

"Why don't you go take a nap?" TJ inclined his head toward the suite's bedroom door. "It's already been a long day."

She glanced at her watch. It was just after four, but to her body, it felt like it could have easily been well after midnight. "If I sleep now, I won't be able to sleep later tonight."

"And if you run yourself ragged, you won't be any help to me, Mark, or yourself. Take a quick nap. I'll wake you in an hour."

A second uncontrollable yawn wiped away all of her remaining hesitation. "Okay. Wake me up in one hour."

TJ held up three fingers. "Scout's honor."

She fell asleep quickly, but her rest was fitful. She awoke ten minutes before the hour was up. The suite's bathroom was a Jack-and-Jill style that had a door opening into the bedroom and a second entrance from the living area.

She could hear TJ moving behind the closed bathroom door.

Her stomach grumbled, and she padded barefoot from the bedroom to the small kitchenette area that housed a coffee maker and, she hoped, something she could snack on while she waited for TJ to emerge from the bathroom so they could discuss dinner plans. She grabbed the bag of peanuts, cringing at the $4.50 price tag before ripping the bag open. She made her way to the sofa, popped a handful of peanuts in her mouth, and froze.

TJ had left the door cracked slightly open. His back was to her and from where she stood, she knew he couldn't see her. But she could see him. Nearly all of him. He was shaving, wearing nothing but a white bath towel around his waist. The dark brown skin of his back was corded in muscles that flexed as he drew his razor along his jaw.

She tried to make herself walk away, head back into the

bedroom before he found her staring at him like a museum exhibit, but she couldn't make her feet move.

TJ turned on the faucet and bent forward, washing the remaining shaving cream from his face, and her mouth went dry while her pulse raced.

Whatever thought of moving along she'd had fled, and she stared openly now.

TJ reached for the hand towel on the counter, his eyes catching hers in the mirror, finally breaking her out of the lust-filled stupor she seemed to have fallen into.

Heat flushed her face, while embarrassment at being caught ogling him climbed in her chest.

"Sorry, I woke up. Hungry. Peanuts." She held the bag up as embarrassment continued to heat her cheeks.

The corners of TJ's mouth turned up, only heightening her embarrassment.

"I'm just going to…" She turned and rushed to the bedroom, shutting the door, then leaning against it.

It had been a long time since she'd felt such a strong burst of desire for a man. Well, technically she couldn't recall ever having felt that strong a desire, not even when she'd been in the two relationships she would have defined as serious over the years. But TJ Roman was not a man she should be desiring. He wasn't a man who stuck, even with a faulty relationship meter. She knew that.

"Pull yourself together," she whispered to herself. She couldn't stay in the bedroom all night. Her stomach was already grumbling that the peanuts weren't nearly enough.

"He's just a man." An incredibly handsome, smart, sexy man.

She took a deep breath and let it out slowly before opening the door again.

TJ was fully dressed now and sitting at the small table adjacent to the kitchenette. The small smile was still on his lips, and the glint in his eyes sent another wave of heat to her cheeks.

"Sorry about that." She walked toward the sofa in the living room.

"No problem. I didn't realize the door had opened. The lock appears to be a little hinky, so watch out for that."

"Yeah, I will. I'm starving. Do you have something in mind for dinner?"

TJ cocked his head to one side. "I saw a Mexican place on the drive here. It's only a couple of blocks away. We can walk."

It was a short walk, but she was nearly ravenous by the time they got to the restaurant. Mexican music played softly while they waited for the hostess to ready their table. Alexis noted that the interior design of the space was somewhat more romantic than the outside would lead patrons to believe. Short candles and a single red rose formed centerpieces on each of the tables, and most were set for two.

The hostess sat them at a table in the center of the restaurant and the waitress wasted no time coming to take their orders.

Alexis munched on the tortilla chips the waitress left while she and TJ waited for their food to be brought out. "Mexican is my favorite."

"I remember," TJ said.

Mark and TJ had done everything they could to discourage her from tagging along with them when they were younger, so she was surprised that TJ would remember something as mundane as her favorite type of food.

"I remember that Christmas that Mark saved up and

bought you that churro maker and your mother was afraid you'd burn down the apartment building."

Alexis laughed. "I'd forgotten about that."

"Mark started saving in June to have enough money to get you something you'd love for Christmas."

Her heart clenched, grief mingling with the memory of the happiness she'd felt when she'd opened that long-ago gift. She'd never share another Christmas with her brother.

"Hey." TJ reached across the table and took her hand in his. "I'm sorry. I didn't mean to make you sad. I shouldn't have brought it up."

"It's not your fault. Sometimes it hits me out of nowhere that I'm all alone now. I have no one."

He squeezed her hand. "You have me. You can always count on me for anything."

The spark of desire she'd felt earlier as she'd watched him shave returned, even stronger than it had been. She had the urge to lean forward and press her lips against his mouth, to see what he tasted like.

Before she could do anything foolish that she'd certainly regret, the waitress returned with their meals.

They settled in to eat, making small talk and catching up on what had happened in their lives since they'd last seen each other. By the time the waitress cleared their plates, Alexis found that she'd relaxed completely and was enjoying TJ's company.

"You up for sharing a couple of churros? I still have a weakness for them." Alexis reached for the dessert menu the waitress had left at the corner of their table.

"No, I think we should head back to the hotel. Now," TJ answered, his expression serious. His attention trained over her shoulder.

Alexis turned and followed the line of TJ's gaze.

Two men sat at a table on the opposite side of the restaurant. One was slender and balding, the other huskier with a dark mustache. Nothing in particular stood out about them to Alexis, but it was clear that something had for TJ.

The husky man glanced at their table, looking away quickly when his eyes met Alexis's.

"Let's go," TJ said, dropping enough money on the table to more than cover the check.

Alexis stood, letting TJ grasp her elbow gently and lead her to the restaurant doors.

As they hurried along the sidewalk back to the hotel, TJ looking over his shoulder every few steps, apprehension grew in Alexis's gut.

"Do you really think those guys were watching us?"

"I don't know." TJ turned to look behind them again while continuing to move along the sidewalk. It wasn't late, but there weren't very many people out and about.

Alexis glanced over her shoulder but didn't see either of the men.

"Maybe you're overreacting," she said with a note of hopefulness.

"Maybe."

But she could tell by his tone that he didn't think so.

They made it back to the hotel and to their suite.

TJ led her inside, then turned back for the door. "I'm going to circle the perimeter, make sure they didn't follow us or aren't waiting for us to fall asleep. You stay here. Do not open the door to anyone. I'll be back in less than ten minutes. If anything goes wrong, call Shawn, understand?"

She nodded, not trusting the words to work around the fear lodged in her throat.

TJ disappeared out the door and she remained rooted in place. But not for long.

Moments after TJ stepped out of the room, footsteps pounded on the exterior stairs. She heard TJ's deep voice order, "Stop right there."

She crossed the suite to the window overlooking the courtyard and pulled back the heavy curtain.

Two men with masks pulled low over their faces stood at the top of the step, facing TJ. They had the same build as the men from the restaurant, but there was no way to know for sure if it was them.

Alexis's heart raced as the husky guy lunged for TJ.

She raced for the door, pulling it open despite TJ's admonition not to open it until he returned.

TJ grabbed the man's arm, wrenching it behind his back as he brought his knee up to meet the man's chin. The husky man flew backward into the door of one of the other hotel rooms with a grunt. He slid down the door, one hand pressed to his chest, his breath coming in ragged gasps.

The taller, slender man came at TJ, his punch landing on TJ's jaw and sending him stumbling. The slender man didn't waste any time raining more punches down.

Alexis glanced around for something to use to help, but before she found a weapon, a door opened farther along the corridor.

A woman with large blonde curls stepped out, and seeing the melee, screamed for help.

The slender man froze, his gaze pulled toward the screaming woman.

TJ lurched to his feet, headbutting the slender man and sending him crashing into the railing that stopped him from falling onto the pavers below. TJ threw a punch to the man's jaw, followed by a kick to his gut that took the man down to his knees.

More doors opened along the corridor.

An elderly man peeked his head out of his room, then yelled that he was calling the police.

The huskier man finally made it to his feet. "Let's go," he huffed.

The slender man was still on his knees. He looked up at TJ, hostility shooting from his eyes like laser beams.

"Come on!" The husky man had already started down the staircase.

The slender man held TJ's gaze for a moment longer before getting to his feet and following his friend.

Alexis ran to TJ's side. "You're just going to let them leave?"

TJ's gaze didn't waver from the men. They jumped into a dark sedan and peeled away from the hotel parking lot.

"Yes," he said. "I can't leave you to chase after them. They might just be a distraction."

Icy fear snaked through her. The distraction. That meant that there could be someone else out there coming for them.

TJ threw his arm around her and hustled her back to the room.

"Hey, wait a minute. You need to report those guys to the cops," one of the other hotel guests called out to their backs.

TJ ignored the man, hustling her into their suite and securing the door.

"We need to get out of here. You should go pack up."

Alexis grabbed a napkin from beside the coffee maker and pressed it to TJ's bleeding lip. "We aren't going to report this to the police?"

"I think we will probably have to since I had an audience, but I'm going to tell them that I think those guys were just trying to mug me."

"But you don't think that, really?" Alexis pulled the napkin from TJ's lip, eliciting a grimace of pain. "Sorry."

"It's fine." He waved off her attempt to press the napkin against his split lip again. "No, I don't. I'm pretty sure those were the same guys watching us at the restaurant, and since I know they didn't follow us as we walked back to the hotel, that means they know where we're staying."

"How is that possible?"

"I don't know, but I'm going to find out."

Chapter Eleven

The police were at the hotel for more than an hour, taking his and Alexis's statement, as well as the statements of the neighboring hotel guests who'd witnessed the fight. He'd avoided lying when he recounted the details of the attack, but he hadn't told the officers about the break-in at Alexis's or why they were in Virginia. The officers pretty clearly believed they'd been victims of a crime of convenience, an attempted robbery gone wrong, and his instincts told him it was best to let them believe that for now. It appeared as if the statements of the other hotel guests supported that belief. The officer who'd taken his statement handed TJ his card and informed him that he could request a copy of the incident report in seventy-two hours. He held out little hope that anything would come of the police investigation. No one had been seriously injured and the would-be muggers had gotten away with nothing.

He closed the suite door behind the last officer and turned to Alexis. She looked exhausted. He'd have loved to give her a few hours to get some rest. Hell, he'd have loved to get a few hours of sleep himself, but it was too risky. Those guys could come back with reinforcements. They needed to move now.

"You were amazing fighting off those guys," Alexis

said with a small smile, despite the fatigue that shone in her eyes.

"Thanks. And I'm sorry to do this to you, but we have to get moving. We can't stay here."

"I know. Those guys might have just been a distraction," she said, repeating what he said earlier. She shivered.

"Hey." He reached out and pulled her to him before he realized he was doing it. "Don't worry. I'm not going to let anyone get to you."

"Do you think the cops bought your story about those guys being muggers?" she asked, her face pressed against his chest.

He knew she could hear his heart beating and wondered if she realized that its pace had more than doubled since she'd stepped into his arms.

"They bought it. They want to buy it. They've got bigger issues to deal with than an attempted mugging. Especially one where the muggers got away with nothing of value."

"But don't you think it might be better for us if we explained about Mark's death and our investigation?" She pulled away just enough that she could look up at him. "Maybe with the mugging and the attack in my home, the detective in charge of the case will see that there is something very wrong going on here and take my claim that Mark couldn't have committed suicide more seriously."

TJ considered the idea. "Maybe, but I'd like to meet the detective first. Feel her out a bit before we start sharing information."

"I guess that makes sense." Alexis stepped out of his arms and he fought the intense desire to pull her back against him again.

Where she belongs. The thought popped into his head,

but he was more surprised by the fact that he didn't want to swat it back.

"Are you all packed?" he asked, focusing on what needed to be done and ignoring his libido for now.

"Yes, I packed while you finished up with the police officer. I'm ready to go." Alexis turned and disappeared into the bedroom.

"Good. Me too." In fact, he'd never unpacked. It wouldn't be the first time, and probably not the last, that he'd lived out of a bag.

He took Alexis's bag from her and slung it onto one shoulder, then hiked his own bag on the other.

"We'll call Shawn from the car and let him know what happened. I was able to get a partial plate from the car those guys drove off in, but I don't know how much help it will be. Chances are the car is a rental or more likely stolen, but if anyone can track it down, it's Shawn."

TJ opened the door, scanning the area before waving for Alexis to step out of the room. They walked quickly to the car while he remained on alert. He doubted the guys would return to the hotel so soon, but there'd now been two attempts to get to Alexis, which meant she made a motivated enemy.

"What I don't understand is how those guys knew we were staying at this hotel," Alexis said as they hurried to the rental car. "I mean, you were looking the whole time we made our way back to the hotel from the restaurant and there are more than a half dozen other hotels in this area."

"That's a good question." TJ contemplated the answer as he beeped the SUV's trunk open and placed their bags inside. "Get in. I want to check something."

He waited until Alexis had gotten in on the passenger

side and closed and locked the door before walking around the SUV. He ran his hand over the inside of each of the wheel wells. Behind the front driver's side tire, he found what he was looking for.

Alexis lowered the passenger window as he approached. "What is that?"

"A GPS tracker. That's why they didn't have to follow us from the restaurant. They knew where to find us."

He took several photos of the tracker before tossing it to the pavement and stomping on it. In a perfect world, he'd have a West technician examine it to see if they couldn't get some information off it that might tell them who'd bought it or planted it on the car, but he couldn't take the chance of taking it with them while it was still emitting a signal notifying their pursuers of where they were going next. The photos were going to have to do.

He rounded the car and hopped into the driver's side. He peeled out of the parking lot before instructing the in-phone assistant to call Shawn West.

It took several minutes to update Shawn.

"You two are okay, though, right?" Shawn asked once TJ had finished explaining the night's events.

"We're fine. I've got a split lip and will probably have one hell of a shiner tomorrow, but I've had worse," TJ answered. He didn't know where they were going, but driving aimlessly wasn't a bad idea at the moment. It made it easier to spot if they had a tail. So far, they were in the clear.

"What do you need from me?" Shawn asked.

"A secure place to sleep would be great." TJ glanced across the car. Alexis had looked exhausted before, but she was all but wilting now. Her head rested against the back of the seat and her eyes were closed, although he knew she wasn't asleep.

"No problem. I actually have a buddy who lives in Virginia. It's not too far from where you are. He's overseas right now, but he's let me use his place as a safe house before."

"That's some good friend."

Shawn chuckled. "Yeah, well, he's in the business, too." The business being the business of elite private security, TJ knew. "Give me a minute to reach out."

Ryan West had once told him that more than being a skilled fighter or being able to hack into computer systems or even anticipating potential dangers, private security and investigations were about contacts. Knowing the right people and being able to call on them when you needed to. That seemed to be proving true now.

"Okay, my buddy says the place is empty, and it's fine for you and Alexis to stay there as long as you need to," Shawn told TJ.

Shawn came back on the line after several minutes. He relayed the address and the details of how to gain entry into the house. TJ was to call a phone number when they arrived and Shawn's friend would unlock the door remotely for them. The joys of technology.

It took about an hour for them to get to the house, but as Shawn had promised, they had no trouble getting in touch with his friend and getting inside. TJ took a quick tour around the home, which he noted was quite nice, before walking Alexis to the room he'd deemed safest for her to claim.

He placed her bag on the bed and was headed for the door when she placed a hand on his biceps, stopping him.

"Just in case I haven't said it before, thank you. For being here with me. For believing me. For protecting me."

He reached out a hand and palmed her cheek. "I will always be here for you, and I will always protect you."

She took a step forward, closing the short distance between them. Her flowery perfume tickled his nose and lit the flame of desire in him.

Her eyes closed, and she tilted her head up. Her plump lips were the most enticing thing he'd ever seen, and it took every punch of willpower he had to force himself to step away from her.

"I'll be across the hall if you need me."

Alexis's eyes opened, reflecting the same confusion mixed with the desire he felt inside.

Falling into bed with her now would be a mistake. An admittedly enjoyable mistake, but still, a mistake. And he couldn't afford any mistakes now. Not when Alexis's life could be on the line.

Chapter Twelve

TJ awoke the next morning to a quiet house. He peeked in on Alexis and found her still asleep. The safe house had three full bathrooms and a half bath, so there was no need for him and Alexis to share here.

He set the water to freezing and climbed into the shower.

He'd managed to keep the desire he felt for Alexis every time he looked at her at bay during the day, but he couldn't stop the erotic scenes that had plagued his dreams during the night. He'd awoken hard as a rock and even grumpier than usual. Hence the cold shower. Unfortunately, it wasn't working as well as he'd hoped. He couldn't stop thinking about the hunger he'd seen in her eyes last night when he'd almost kissed her. He'd been with enough women to know that look when he saw it. She'd wanted him as much as he'd wanted her.

Yet he'd still pulled away.

It was the right thing to do.

So then why didn't it feel right?

He turned the shower nozzle from cold to scalding, hoping the hot water would finish the work of quelling his growing feelings for Alexis.

He'd been right to stop what was clearly going to be a mistake for both of them. Alexis wasn't a woman he could jump into bed with just for fun, even if she agreed to it. He cared about her, more than he liked to admit, certainly more than any woman he'd ever dated. She deserved the white picket fence, two kids, and a husband whose job didn't involve living out of a car for days on end so he could catch other married people cheating on their spouses. It was more than he could, or was willing, to give. So he needed to put his libido in park and focus on the task at hand.

He turned off the water and stepped out of the shower.

He and Alexis still had a lot of work to do if they had any chance of proving that Mark didn't steal TalCon's software program and even more work ahead of them when it came to proving Mark didn't commit suicide. All of which was made more difficult by the fact that he had almost no idea what he was doing.

He got dressed in jeans and a gray pullover while considering, for probably the hundredth time since he'd agreed to take on Alexis's case, whether he'd serve her better by letting Shawn or nearly anyone else at West take the lead. He chased cheaters, deadbeat dads, and disability fraudsters. He didn't know the first thing about software programs and military contracts. And proving that Mark was really murdered?

He stopped himself before his thoughts really began to spiral and took a deep breath, letting it out slowly.

Alexis had come to him and he wasn't going to let her down or pawn her off on someone else. This may not have been his usual type of case, but any good investigator knew that information was key.

Which was why he'd emailed Shawn to ask him to pull background reports on Nelson Bacon and Arnold Forrick after Alexis went to bed last night. And after some internal debate, he'd also asked Shawn to pull a background report on Mark, although doing so had left him feeling as if he was betraying his friend. Still, it had been nearly two years since he'd spoken to Mark. And if their last encounter was any indication, Mark's drinking was worse than TJ had realized. Maybe he didn't know his friend as well as he thought he did. It was possible Mark had gotten himself into something, wittingly or unwittingly, that he didn't know how to get out of. Even though checking into Mark made him feel guilty, as if he was betraying his friend, he couldn't ignore the possibility that the situation was just what the cops and TalCon said it was. Not that he would say that to Alexis unless and until he had concrete proof that her brother was a thief who had ended his own life rather than face the consequences of his actions.

In the kitchen, he popped two of the frozen muffins he'd found in the freezer into the toaster oven and started a pot of coffee before opening his laptop.

He clicked on the email from Shawn that was waiting at the top of his inbox just as his cell phone rang.

"Good timing," TJ answered the phone. "I was just opening up the email with the background reports. Thanks for doing that, by the way."

"Not a problem," Shawn responded. "I told you I've got your back on this. Whatever you need."

TJ skimmed the report. "Has Tansy made any headway on tracing the person who made the posting for Nimbus on the dark web?"

Shawn sighed. "Not so far."

TJ beat back a surge of frustration and focused on the email Shawn had sent him. "I'm just getting a look at these reports. Is there anything in here about Bacon or Forrick I should focus on?"

"Both these guys are good at what they do. Both ex-military. Both highly decorated. Bacon was a Ranger. Forrick a Marine. Doesn't appear they knew each other in the service, but they both landed at TalCon about the same time and rose in the ranks pretty much in lockstep. Bacon is the better diplomat, which propelled him to the top seat as CEO, but he brought Forrick along as his right-hand man. Forrick is the heavy. He does whatever Bacon needs him to do, leaving Bacon's hands relatively clean."

"Not a bad setup."

"No, and there's nothing I could find that suggests either of them is anything other than your typical, sometimes ruthless, corporate executive."

The toaster dinged. TJ put the phone on speaker and carried it with him while he fixed himself a cup of coffee and buttered his muffin. "I've been thinking about the theft of the software. Atwal, the lawyer Mark hired to represent him, said that TalCon's cybersecurity professionals found an offer to sell the program on the dark web. I don't think this is the first rodeo for whoever stole this program."

"You think the thief has done this before?"

"This or something like it. Whoever this is knows way too much about TalCon and this program and how to offload it for this to be the first time they've done this."

"Yeah, but you'd think that if someone were running around stealing computer programs that could be used to wage cyber war, it would make the news."

"Not necessarily. Atwal said that one of the reasons that Mark hadn't been charged was that TalCon is still hoping to recover the program without a lot of fanfare. Maybe this kind of theft has happened previously and TalCon, or whatever company fell victim, worked to keep things just as quiet."

"That makes some sense." Shawn still sounded skeptical. "I'll dig around. See what I can find."

"Thanks. Hopefully, it will generate some much needed leads that don't point back to Mark."

TJ let his cursor hang over the third and final report Shawn had attached to the email. Mark's background report.

"How is Alexis?" Shawn asked.

"Hanging in there. She's strong. She'll get through this."

"How about you? I was surprised to see you asked for a background on your friend. Are you starting to have doubts?"

Was he? He didn't doubt the Mark he'd known would never have done what he was being accused of. But the Mark who thought he'd ever make a play for his woman. The Mark that was drinking heavily the last time TJ had seen him. He wasn't sure he knew that Mark at all.

"Just being thorough." It seemed a safe enough answer, but Shawn was too good of an investigator not to have heard the hesitation.

"I sent the photos of the tracker to our technology team. I'll let you know what, if anything, they are able to find out."

"Thanks. Sorry I couldn't get the actual device to you, but I didn't want to take any chances."

"I get it. I don't want to step on your toes, but have you checked for other devices? That might not have been the only one."

"I did a thorough check of the car last night. Didn't find anything else, but you know this kind of investigation isn't really what I'm used to doing."

"You're doing fine. And like I said, I got your back. And to prove it, after I pulled the backgrounds on Forrick and Bacon, I dug around some more." The laptop chimed with an incoming email. "TalCon's a juggernaut in the military contracting world, but they have a couple of upstart competitors nipping at their heels. I figured it might be worth looking at who would benefit if TalCon does a very public and embarrassing face-plant with Nimbus."

The new email contained research on TalCon's two closest competitors. TJ kicked himself for not having thought of the competition angle himself. "Thanks, man."

"No problem. I'm also sending you a name."

TJ's email chimed again. The name Noel Muscarelli followed by an address. The text also included Noel's phone number.

"Noel Muscarelli is a former executive at TalCon who abruptly left the company six months ago, even though he'd been touted as one of Bacon's possible successors."

TJ was surprised by Shawn's last statement. "Is Bacon on his way out?"

"Umm… That's an open question. Bacon has been in the CEO chair for twelve years. At some point, probably in the not-too-distant future, the board is going to have to start thinking about who follows him."

"What about Forrick?"

"Uh-uh." TJ imagined Shawn shaking his head on the other end of the line. "Forrick has burned too many bridges getting and keeping Bacon on top. When Bacon goes, Forrick goes too."

Footsteps sounded down the hall where the bedrooms were. Alexis was awake.

"Thanks, Shawn. This is great. It gives me a few bushes to beat in hopes that something falls out."

TJ ended the call as Alexis entered the kitchen. She wore a pink T-shirt and pink pajama shorts that showed enough of her tantalizingly creamy caramel skin to have him considering taking yet another cold shower.

"Good morning."

"Good morning."

"I made coffee and thawed out a muffin for you."

"Thanks." She turned away from him quickly and he saw her cheeks pink. "I thought I heard you talking to someone."

"Shawn. I asked him to do some background research for me." TJ filled her in on the conversation. "Shawn found a former TalCon employee who worked in the same section as Mark who might be worth tracking down."

"That sounds great. Speaking of TalCon employees, has Lenora Kenda gotten back to you?"

TJ frowned. "No." Ms. Kenda was proving elusive, and he didn't like it. There was no reason for Mark's assistant to dodge his call unless she was hiding something. She was definitely on his list of people to talk to sooner rather than later. "I think it's time we try being more forward with Miss Kenda. I want to take a drive by her house today. See if we can't get her to chat with us. But I think it might be best to reach out to Noel Muscarelli, the former TalCon employee, first. He's more likely to talk to us since he's no longer with TalCon, and we still need to chat with Detective Chellel. We also need to track down Mark's ex, Jessica."

Alexis carried her coffee mug to the table and sat. "Mark told me they'd broken up a few weeks before he died. I'm not sure she'd know anything that could help us."

"We won't know until we ask."

Alexis frowned.

"I know you didn't like your brother's taste in women. But this is part of investigating. Following all the potential leads, even the ones that don't look as if they will pan out to anything."

Alexis held up her hands in surrender. "You're right. You're the expert. If you say we need to talk to Jessica, we talk to Jessica."

TJ didn't feel like an expert, but Jessica was clearly someone they needed to speak to. "Tansy got Jessica's most recent address. I thought we would pay her a visit this morning before stopping by the police station to talk to Detective Chellel. I'm going to call Noel Muscarelli and see if we can arrange to meet up sometime today."

"Wow, I'm impressed. You got all that done before I even got out of bed."

Pride swelled in TJ's chest at her compliment. "It wasn't that much, but you better hurry and get dressed if we want to get a jump on this day."

Alexis downed the remainder of her coffee, then hurried back up the stairs.

He called Noel Muscarelli while Alexis showered and changed. Noel agreed to meet with them at noon at a small coffee shop not far from his home.

After ending the call, TJ's gaze fell on the email from Shawn that contained the background on Mark. He hadn't opened it. Yet. Once again, his finger hovered over the keyboard, but the sound of Alexis heading back toward the kitchen stopped him.

He closed the laptop and turned, forcing a smile. "Ready to go?"

Alexis returned his smile with a tepid one of her own. "Ready as I'll ever be."

They set out for Jessica Castaldo's apartment complex. The two-story brown boxy building was utilitarian, but it looked well kept.

TJ knocked on the door of apartment 2B and got no answer. He knocked a second time just as the door to apartment 2A was flung open.

"Ain't nobody there." A rail-thin woman with gray hair in two braids that stopped just above her buttocks stood in the open door of the opposite apartment.

Alexis and TJ turned to face the woman, who gave Alexis a quick once-over, but her gaze lingered on TJ. A smile, likely meant to be seductive, quirked her mouth up.

TJ noted, with more than a little satisfaction, that Alexis's lips had taken a decidedly downward turn. She scowled at Jessica's neighbor.

Thinking it was best that he take the lead, he smiled at the woman and said, "Hi there. We're looking for your neighbor, Jessica Castaldo."

The woman smiled back at TJ. "I never knew what her name was, but she doesn't live there anymore. Moved out a couple weeks ago."

"Did she say where she was going?" Alexis asked, a polite smile replacing her former scowl .

The woman shot Alexis a disinterested look before turning her attention back to TJ. "No idea. She didn't exactly leave a forwarding address with me. Like I said, I never even knew her name. A real standoffish little thing, she was."

"Well, could you tell us how long she lived here?"

The woman waved her hand dismissively. "Oh, about six months. Not long. I know she didn't give thirty days' notice like we're all supposed to do if we're going to move out. Super was fit to be tied. Asked me a bunch of questions about where she went, just like you're doing. And I told him the same thing. I didn't really know Little Miss Thing."

TJ pulled out his cell phone and put up a picture of Mark. "Did you ever see her with this man?" He turned the phone to face the woman.

The woman squinted at the screen for a moment. "Yeah, yeah. I've seen him around here a few times. Not for a few weeks before Little Miss Thing moved out. I think they were dating, but he must've gotten wise and broken up with her."

"What did he get wise to?" Alexis pressed.

The woman jutted her chin in the direction of Jessica's apartment door. "She was a gold digger. Had a job as a waitress or something. I've seen her in her uniform. But no waitressing job is gonna pay for Jimmy Choo shoes and Fendi bags and all those expensive clothes I'd see her traipsing off to the club in on Saturday nights."

For someone who didn't even know her neighbor's name, the woman sure had seen a lot of the goings-on at Jessica's place.

"Is there anything else you can tell us about your neighbor? Anything that might help us figure out where she moved to?"

To her credit, the woman did seem to think about it for a moment before shaking her head. "Naw, I just told you everything I know about her."

TJ put his phone back in his pocket and shot the woman another smile. "Thanks for your help."

The woman smiled back at him. "You're welcome. Anytime, handsome. If you want to come in, maybe have a drink or two?"

TJ heard the soft growl emanating from Alexis's throat. If the other woman heard it, she gave no indication.

"Sorry," TJ said, placing a hand on Alexis's back and guiding her toward the staircase. "I'm on the clock."

"Too bad."

He heard the sound of the woman's door closing.

"I can wait in the car if you want to get to know your new friend a little better," Alexis groused.

TJ's lips twisted into a smile he was sure wasn't going to make his situation any better. He was right. Alexis's scowl deepened when she saw it.

He opened the door to the car and slid in behind the wheel. Alexis slid in next to him.

"Hey, I can't help it if women find me attractive," he joked, hoping to lighten the mood in the car.

Alexis's lips quirked up slightly. "I'll bet. But your attractiveness didn't do much to help us. We have no idea where Jessica lives."

TJ started the car. "No, but I'm not about to let that stop us. I'll give Shawn a call and see if he can dig up Jessica's new address. But right now, we have a meeting with the detective."

Chapter Thirteen

Alexis didn't read happiness on the face of Detective Elaine Chellel when she walked into the police precinct and found Alexis and TJ in the waiting room. Detective Chellel was a tall, wide-framed woman with blonde hair that was shot through with gray. She wore a dark brown pantsuit, no makeup and a scowl. Alexis had done a bit of checking into Detective Chellel following her interview with the woman after Mark's death. She knew the detective was married with two kids and had spent time on the San Francisco police force before moving to Alexandria, Virginia, several years earlier. In their prior conversations, Chellel had displayed a no-nonsense direct approach, which Alexis might have appreciated more if the detective hadn't been telling her that Mark was suspected of theft and having committed suicide. She'd found several articles lauding her for having closed difficult cases, including homicides. She had hoped that meant the detective would have an open mind, but based on their past interactions, that didn't appear to be the case.

Their first conversation had been rather informal, the detective extending her condolences and asking general questions about Mark. But their second interaction had been much more pointed. More of an interrogation, really.

The detective had wanted to know everything Alexis knew about Mark's work at TalCon. Since she and Mark hadn't spoken to each other in several weeks, and work was rarely a topic of conversation when they did, Alexis hadn't been able to help the detective much.

The detective had not been happy.

Detective Chellel had seemed all in on the theory that Mark had stolen from TalCon and taken his own life as the walls closed in around him. Alexis's calls requesting updates on Mark's case had, at first, been met with the perfunctory statement that the "investigation was ongoing." Detective Chellel hadn't bothered returning her last several messages at all.

Alexis introduced TJ as a family friend and private investigator. Detective Chellel excused herself from the room, leaving Alexis and TJ to take seats around the circular conference room table.

She was back a moment later with a thick file folder under her arm. "Miss Douglas, I'm surprised to see you here. What can I do for you?" Detective Chellel said, as she took a seat.

"You haven't responded to my last messages, so I thought I'd pay a visit. I'd like to know if there's been any progress in my brother's case."

Frown lines formed on Detective Chellel's forehead. "As I explained to you the last time we spoke, every indication we have is that your brother took his own life. I know that's hard to hear—"

"It's not hard to hear, Detective. It's utterly impossible to believe. Mark had hired a lawyer. He denied the accusations of theft against him and he was prepared to fight to prove his innocence."

"Be that as it may—"

"Detective, I think there is something else you should know," TJ interrupted. "Alexis was attacked in her home a few nights ago."

Concern flashed across the detective's face. "I'm sorry to hear that. Did you report the assault?"

"I did," Alexis responded. "Although I'm not sure that the Newark cops took my claims any more seriously than you have."

Detective Chellel frowned. "I'm sure they will do a thorough job of investigating."

"The assailant threatened Alexis," TJ said. "Specifically, warning her to back off looking into Mark's death."

Detective Chellel slipped a notepad from beneath the file and took a pen from her jacket pocket. "Take me through everything that happened."

Alexis did as asked. Detective Chellel listened attentively, asking a handful of questions but mostly letting Alexis go through the break-in. When she got to the part about the assailant's threats, Detective Chellel pressed her. Did she recognize the voice? Was there anything at all distinctive about it? Was she sure about what the man had said?

The detective tapped her pen against the table for several long moments after she'd exhausted all her questions. "I'm not sure how the break-in at your home fits into my investigation. I have entertained the possibility that your brother had an accomplice, especially since we haven't yet recovered the stolen property."

Ire rose in Alexis's gut. "An accomplice? The man who assaulted me is most likely the real thief, not an accomplice. He's framing my brother. That's why he doesn't want me looking into things. That's why he killed…" She choked on the rest of the words.

"Miss Douglas," Detective Chellel said, sliding a little closer in her rolling chair. "I'm afraid there are quite a few things we've turned up that your brother didn't tell you about his life. I'm not at liberty to share everything, as this is still an ongoing investigation, but you may not like what I am able to tell you."

Apprehension tingled down Alexis's spine. "I want to hear it. Whatever it is."

The detective sighed. "It seems your brother had racked up quite a bit of debt."

"That can't be right. I know Mark made a good salary at TalCon. He told me that he'd almost finished paying off his student loans and that he was saving to buy a house. He was very responsible with his money."

Chellel took a sheet of paper from the folder and slid it across the table to Alexis. Mark's bank statement. Line after line showed withdrawals. One to two hundred dollars at first, then the withdrawals got bigger. Five hundred. One thousand. Sixteen hundred. Mark was bleeding money.

"What is this? Where is all this money going?" Alexis looked up from the statement at Detective Chellel.

"I've talked to several of Mark's friends and coworkers. Your brother had developed a gambling problem."

Alexis gripped the arm of her chair. "No. I…he never said anything to me about gambling." She vaguely remembered Mark saying something about going to a local casino for a bachelor party weekend with some friends several months earlier. But one weekend with the boys couldn't turn a person into a gambling addict.

Detective Chellel gave her a sympathetic look. "It's not

uncommon for something like this to be kept from family members and loved ones. Either the person doesn't think they have a problem or they are too embarrassed to seek help for it. His bank statements show numerous withdrawals from an ATM in the MGM National Harbor."

There were dozens of highlighted lines showing withdrawals in the pages that Detective Chellel handed Alexis. Struggling to make sense of what the detective was saying to her, she handed the bank statement to TJ.

Alexis struggled for a moment to grab onto a nugget of information that was pushing its way into the forefront of her mind. "The MGM? Isn't that where Jessica Castaldo works?" She recalled now that Jessica had mentioned working there when she and Mark had visited.

Detective Chellel nodded. "Yes. When I spoke to her, she said that was how she and Mark met." Detective Chellel pulled a photo out of the file she'd brought into the room. "We also discovered that your brother had been prescribed diazepam for stress and anxiety by his doctor."

She slid the photo across the table to Alexis. It showed a close-up of an empty prescription bottle with Mark's name on the label.

"The empty bottle we found in his apartment was his own prescription," the detective continued. "We've also developed information that suggests your brother had a drinking problem. A problem you never mentioned when we spoke about your brother in our earlier interviews, Miss Douglas." Chellel's tone was pointed.

Alexis caught the glance TJ shot her way. "It didn't seem relevant. Mark drank too much, yes. But he'd never hurt himself or others."

Mark's DUI and TJ's description of how out of control

Mark had been on the night their friendship had fractured played through her mind, but she wouldn't let the detective define Mark by his worst moments.

"This account shows a negative balance." TJ's voice brought her back to the present. "How was Mark paying his bills with this much money going out, presumably to feed his gambling?"

Chellel shook her head. "He wasn't. His landlord says he was always late with the rent and often short on money. The financing company for his car had already started the repossession process."

Alexis massaged the growing headache behind her temples. "This is madness."

"I'm sure it's hard to make sense of now," Detective Chellel said.

"So you think Mark's gambling losses were the catalyst for the theft?" TJ asked the detective.

Chellel nodded. "That looks to be the case. We know Mark downloaded the completely updated program a few days before an online posting went up on the dark web offering its sale."

"Mark was working on the program. His downloading it isn't suspicious," Alexis said.

"His coworkers at TalCon say the work he was doing on the program would not have required him to download it. And the system shows that it was downloaded to an external drive. That is expressly prohibited by company policy according to the people we spoke with."

Frustration bubbled in Alexis's chest. She gripped the arms of her chair tighter.

TJ covered her hand with one of his. A warning to keep her cool.

"Have you been able to trace that posting back to Mark?" he asked the detective.

Detective Chellel frowned. "No. It's incredibly difficult to trace anything on the dark web."

"So you still have no proof Mark made the posting," TJ pressed.

Chellel focused her frown on TJ. "No. But we are sure he is the only person who downloaded the complete program."

Alexis worked to keep the scowl off her face. The detective's eagerness to ignore all the inconsistencies in her theory irked her. "And you don't think it's at all suspicious that TalCon's security cameras were offline on the night the program was stolen?"

"No, I don't," the detective responded forcefully. "The system was down for scheduled maintenance. If anything, that hurts your brother's case. He was one of only a handful of employees privy to the company's routine maintenance schedule."

Alexis had no response for that piece of news, so she simply stewed quietly.

"I know this is not what you want to hear," Detective Chellel said after a moment. "But your brother had the means, motive and opportunity to steal the program."

"Even if you're right and Mark did steal the program— and to be clear I don't accept that, but let's assume we're in some bizarro world—that doesn't mean Mark killed himself."

"The charges he would have faced, corporate espionage, theft, cybersecurity violations, are serious felonies. Some of them are federal. He'd have faced decades in prison. It's not a small thing, and when people feel they have no way out..."

Chellel let the rest of the statement hang unspoken.

"But Mark hadn't even been charged yet. He had a lawyer. He was ready to fight to clear his name. It doesn't make sense that he'd just give up."

Detective Chellel looked as if she was fighting to hold on to her patience.

Alexis didn't care. The detective had been far too willing to jump to conclusions when it came to this case. There didn't seem to be anyone pushing her to examine any lines of inquiry that didn't lead to Mark.

"Look, Miss Douglas, I can see how hard this is for you. I'm sure I would feel the same way if the roles were reversed. But I can't ignore the evidence, and right now, all the evidence leads to the conclusion that Mark Douglas stole property from TalCon and took his own life once his theft became known and his arrest was imminent."

"Was his arrest imminent?" TJ interrupted. "Because that's not how Mark's lawyer understood the situation. He was under the impression that TalCon wanted to get the Nimbus program back but to keep the theft quiet at the same time."

Chellel's narrow-eyed gaze shifted to TJ. "I can't speak to what Mr. Atwal understood, but it's not the policy of this police department to spend valuable resources and working hours investigating with the intention of just letting the crimes we turn up go. I'm confident we would have sought and obtained a warrant for Mark Douglas's arrest."

Detective Chellel's statement hit Alexis like a punch in the chest. Her brother had been on the verge of being arrested. How desperate might that knowledge have made him?

No. She knew Mark. No matter what was happening in his life, he wouldn't have gone as far as suicide.

Alexis surged to her feet. "Well then, you would have been arresting the wrong man. And I'm going to prove it."

Chapter Fourteen

TJ guided Alexis from the police station, his arm lightly at her waist. Her determination with the detective had impressed him and, if he was being completely honest, turned him on a little. There was nothing sexier than a strong woman standing up for what she thought was right. Walking close enough to her now that the flowery scent of her perfume engulfed him wasn't doing anything to cool his desire for her, but Alexis didn't seem to be suffering from the same affliction.

She tapped away on her phone, engrossed in whatever she was doing on it, as they exited the police station. He let her be and focused on getting them back to the car.

"We need to go to the MGM and talk to Jessica," Alexis said as he slid into the driver's seat of the rental and turned over the engine.

"We're supposed to meet with Noel Muscarelli, the former TalCon employee Shawn hooked us up with, remember?"

"I know, I know, but you said that meeting was set for noon. That gives us more than an hour and a half. The MGM is fifteen minutes from here. I don't want to wait any longer to find out what Jessica knows."

TJ pulled out of the parking space and headed for the

garage's exit. "We don't even know if Jessica is at work now. You really didn't know anything about Mark's gambling habit?"

"No, nothing at all. Jessica mentioned that she worked at the MGM when she and Mark came to visit me last year, but I had no idea. I mean, it didn't even cross my mind that Mark…"

"Of course not. Why would it? Okay," TJ said, shifting into the right-hand lane when he saw the sign announcing the entrance ramp for the highway was less than a half mile away. "We'll head to the MGM and see if Jessica is working. At the very least, we might be able to find out when she is working and we can return then."

He drove the fifteen minutes to the casino and paid the exorbitant parking fee for a nearby garage.

The MGM was located at the National Harbor, an area that had undergone an extensive revitalization, some might say gentrification, over the last decade. The décor was elegant and upscale. In addition to the casino and hotel, the space boasted a luxuriously appointed spa, several bars and lounges, retail stores, and a bevy of high-end restaurants.

"This place is gorgeous," Alexis said, craning her neck to take in the splendor of the main entrance.

"Gorgeous and huge," TJ responded. He closed a hand over Alexis's elbow and led her toward the casino floor. "These places usually have a lounge off the casino floor. Our best bet is probably to sit there and get the lay of the land first."

He was right. There was a lounge that overlooked the casino's main floor. A waitress approached only seconds after they'd taken a table that allowed them a clear view of the floor. She took their orders, a club soda for him and sparkling water for Alexis.

Alexis scanned the casino floor. "I don't see Jessica."

"There's no guarantee she's here," TJ said. "For now, we need to look like we're just a couple enjoying our drinks and thinking about losing a little money."

Alexis looked at him. "Couple? I thought you didn't do the couple thing?"

His lips quirked up. "Just this once."

"Lucky me," Alexis replied, her voice husky.

The waitress returned, putting an end to the charged moment. It was just as well. He needed to focus. He'd seen a photo of Jessica Castaldo in the background, information on her that he'd gathered, but that didn't mean it would be easy to spot her. If she was even there, which was still an open question.

A question that must have been lingering on Alexis's mind too. "Maybe we should ask our waitress if Jessica is working today?" She nodded at the waitress's retreating back.

"Alexis Douglas?"

Alexis's gaze shifted over his shoulder.

TJ turned to find a tall Latino man with dark hair that grazed his shoulder headed for them.

The man swept Alexis from her seat and kissed her on each of her cheeks before stepping back and holding her at arm's length. "Muñeca, what are you doing here?"

"Antonio. It's so good to see you. I'm just down for a visit." Alexis said, obviously flustered, but the smile on her face made it clear she was happy to see Antonio, whoever he was.

"Well, this is an amazing surprise, then." Antonio pulled Alexis in for another hug.

TJ stood, jealousy knotting his stomach.

Alexis pulled out of the other man's arms and stepped back. "Antonio, I want you to meet my friend, TJ. TJ, this is Antonio. He and I went to culinary school together."

TJ moved to Alexis's side and shook the hand Antonio extended.

"Are you two staying in the hotel here?" Antonio asked.

"Oh, no. We got a place somewhere else," Alexis said, uncertainty in her eyes.

"Good." Antonio leaned in and lowered his voice. "This place is way overpriced. Trust me, I'm the pastry chef at a restaurant here and you don't want me to tell you the difference between what it costs to make our signature dessert versus what we charge the guests." Antonio laughed good naturedly.

TJ found himself warming to the man even though he was standing much too close to Alexis and looked as if he should be on the cover of a magazine instead of in a kitchen. "You two must stay for lunch. I'm not on duty until later this evening, but I'll make sure the kitchen takes care of you."

Alexis's gaze slid to TJ's face. It was almost as if he could read the thoughts going through her mind. Antonio could be just the person they were looking for to help locate Jessica.

TJ nodded, letting her know he was on board with her asking Antonio about Jessica.

"Antonio, we're not just here to visit." Alexis pulled her phone from her pocket and pulled up the photo of Mark, her, and Jessica. "We're looking for this woman. Jessica Castaldo. She's a cocktail waitress at the casino here and she was dating my brother. It's very important that we speak to her."

Antonio peered at the photo. "I'm sorry, I don't know her. A lot of people work for the hotel and casino. If she's dating your brother, wouldn't he know how to get in touch with her?"

Sadness clouded Alexis's eyes.

"Mark died two months ago," TJ said.

"Oh, muñeca." Antonio clasped his hands together, prayer-like. "I'm so sorry to hear that."

"There are questions." TJ picked up the conversation again when it seemed that Alexis would not. "We'd really like to talk to Jessica, but we don't have a working phone number for her and she's moved out of her apartment. We were hoping to catch her at work."

Antonio made a face. "That might be tricky, but let me see what I can do."

Antonio strode away into an area behind the lounge's bar where their waitress seemed to have also disappeared. TJ and Alexis reclaimed their seats.

Curiosity and jealousy getting the best of him, TJ queried, "Muñeca?"

Alexis's brow arched. "Antonio calls all his female friends muñeca. It means doll in Spanish."

"His friends?"

Alexis's lips turned up into a smile, and he knew she knew he was jealous. "Yes, his friends. Antonio is something of a flirt, but he's been married for I don't know how long. Since before I met him. And he and his wife are sickeningly in love."

"Oh, well, that's nice."

Alexis's grin grew. "It is."

She was still smiling when her gaze shifted over his shoulder again.

He turned to find Antonio heading their way again, this time with a woman in tow. She wore the same basic uniform as their waitress wore, a short black skirt, white top and heels.

"Guys, this is Stacey. Stacey, this is Alexis and her friend TJ." Antonio made the introductions. "Stacey knows Jessica."

"Yeah," Stacey said, looking from Antonio to TJ before her gaze finally landed on Alexis. "She used to work here, but she quit about three weeks ago. Maybe a month. I'm not sure. We don't always work the same shifts."

TJ shared a glance with Alexis. "She quit," he pressed. "You're sure?"

Stacey nodded. "Yeah, absolutely. Our manager was pretty upset. She didn't give notice at all. Just called in right before she was scheduled to start her shift and said she wasn't ever coming back. The rest of us had to cover her shifts for the rest of the week. Made a little extra, but it was annoying just the same."

"Do you have a phone number or address for Jessica?" Alexis asked.

Suspicion clouded Stacey's eyes. "I don't know if I should be giving that kind of information out."

Alexis pulled her phone out of her pocket again and turned it toward Stacey.

"This guy, Mark, he's my brother. He was also dating Jessica. He passed away recently, and he left something for Jessica. I want to make sure she gets it."

TJ managed to stifle his surprise at the lie that fell so

easily from Alexis's mouth, but Antonio frowned. Thankfully, he kept quiet.

The suspicion in Stacey's eyes evaporated. "Oh, I recognize him. Good guy. I'm sorry for your loss."

"You knew my brother?"

Stacey's forehead crinkled. "Knew is too strong. He played here a lot, though, so I served him a bunch of times. Good tipper. Terrible gambler."

"Why do you say that?" TJ pressed.

Stacey threw a glance over her shoulder. But they were the only people in the lounge. Even their waitress had disappeared. "Well, I mean, the deck is stacked against you anyway, right? The house always wins and all that. But some people never really get that through their heads. Winning becomes a challenge they just can't let go of. I mean, that's how it becomes an addiction, right?"

"You're saying my brother was addicted to gambling?"

Stacey shot another quick glance over her shoulder. "You're his sister, so you deserve to know. Some of the gamblers with serious problems, they go to this guy, Chamberly, when the casino stops giving them credit."

"A loan shark?" TJ asked to clarify.

A small gasp escaped Alexis's lips.

Stacey nodded. "I saw your brother talking to him once at a bar down the street. Chamberly is persona non grata in the hotel and casino, so he does his business out of the Blue Bull Bar. I think he owns part of it or part of the owner," she scoffed. "That's all I know."

Stacey didn't have a current phone number or address for Jessica or a full name for Chamberly. She wished them luck before sauntering away.

Antonio reissued his offer for lunch, but they took a

raincheck. They had a half hour to make it back to Alexandria for their meeting with Noel.

TJ paid their bill and he and Alexis began the drive back to Alexandria. He used the speakerphone to call Shawn on the way, briefly updating him on what they'd learned at the casino.

"So could you see if you or Tansy can dig up a current address and phone number for Jessica Castaldo and whatever we can find on this Chamberly? A full name would be great, for starters."

"Chamberly. I've heard of him, although I thought he operated in Atlantic City. I guess the new casino on the harbor was too good of an opportunity for him to pass up. He's a predator," Shawn said with more than a little disgust in his voice.

TJ shot a look across the car at Alexis. "Is he dangerous?"

Shawn grunted. "No more so than any loan shark. Generally, these guys might work a guy over, but murder is bad business. Brings police attention, and dead men don't pay."

Alexis let out a deep breath. "So you don't think he could have killed Mark?"

"I didn't say that, but it's not likely."

"Can you get us a meeting with him?" TJ asked Shawn. The silence on the other side of the line went on and on. "Shawn, are you still there?"

"I'm here. I can reach out to a few people and see what I can do, but are you sure about this?"

"I think we have to talk to him." He glanced at Alexis again, hesitating to say exactly what he was thinking while she was in earshot.

Shawn didn't have any such misgiving. "We have to consider that Mark might have stolen Nimbus as a means of paying off a debt to Chamberly."

"No!" Alexis exclaimed.

"It's a possibility we have to explore," TJ said at the same time.

Alexis shot a look his way. "Mark would never do something like that."

"Sweetheart, there's only one thing we've learned so far, and that is that Mark had a lot of secrets. If you really want to get to the bottom of his death, we have to look into everything."

The interior of the car was quiet for a full minute. Even Shawn remained silent on the open line.

"Fine," Alexis spat finally. "We'll talk to this Chamberly person. We'll turn over every rock and when we do, I know we'll prove Mark's innocence."

TJ hoped for Alexis's sake that would be the case.

Chapter Fifteen

Shawn ended the call with a promise to get back to them as soon as he'd arranged a meeting with Chamberly. Alexis and TJ made the rest of the drive to meet Noel Muscarelli in silence. The weight of being the only one who believed, no, who knew, that Mark was innocent, pressed down on her until she thought she'd break.

TJ found a parking spot in the small, paved lot next to the café. He held the door open and Alexis stepped into the coffee shop where Noel Muscarelli had agreed to meet them. At a little after noon, there were only a handful of tables occupied. The space was small, but she could tell right away that they prepared their own baked goods. The air smelled of sugar and cinnamon. An instrumental pop song she vaguely recognized played too loudly from the overhead speakers.

Noel Muscarelli wasn't hard to spot. He sat alone, a steaming cup in front of him, his eyes trained on the door of the shop.

Alexis moved toward him, with TJ following closely behind. "Noel?" The man nodded. "Hi. I'm Alexis Douglas. Mark's sister. Thank you for agreeing to speak with us."

"No problem." Noel shook her hand, then turned to TJ. "You must be Mr. Roman."

"TJ, please." TJ shook Noel's hand.

"Can I get either of you something to drink?" Noel asked once Alexis and TJ were seated across the table from him.

"We should be extending that offer to you, but no, I'm fine, thank you," Alexis replied.

"I'm okay."

"Oh, okay." Noel tapped his nails against the side of his cup. "Sorry if I'm a little nervous. When you called to say you wanted to talk to me about TalCon… Well, I don't have good memories of that place."

"I'm sure you heard about Mark. His being accused of stealing from TalCon and…" She let the rest of the sentence fall away. She still couldn't bring herself to say that Mark had committed suicide.

"Yes. It was such a shock. I'm truly sorry for your loss." Noel looked at her with sadness in his eyes.

"Thank you. TJ was also close to Mark, and neither one of us believes that Mark would have done what TalCon is saying he did. We're hoping you can help us."

Noel fidgeted in his chair. "I'm not sure how. I haven't worked at TalCon for more than six months now."

"If it's not too forward, you could start by telling us why you left TalCon. I understand that you worked in the same division as Mark," TJ said.

Noel leaned back in his chair, seemingly considering how to reply. Or maybe whether to reply at all. He was silent for so long, Alexis started to think he wasn't going to answer.

"I guess, if you think it would help prove Mark isn't a thief, which, for the record, I don't buy."

Alexis felt her shoulders relax and realized she'd been worried about speaking to Noel. So far, it seemed as if everyone who knew Mark had bought TalCon's story that he'd stolen from them. She didn't realize just how much stress having her brother's name dragged through the mud had put on her.

"I appreciate that." She smiled across the table at Noel.

"I worked at TalCon in the cybersecurity and engineering division with Mark. We were both senior engineers, and we were both assigned to work on a special program that the company was pouring tons of money into."

"Nimbus," Alexis said.

Noel startled in surprise. "Yes. I don't know how you know that…"

"We spoke with Nelson Bacon and Arnold Forrick yesterday, but they were pretty tight-lipped when it came to Nimbus," TJ said. "Can you give us a bit more detail about what exactly it is we're talking about?"

"I don't know," Noel said nervously. "TalCon let me go, but my nondisclosure agreement is still in effect. They were very clear about that as they frog-marched me from the building."

"Noel," Alexis said, leaning forward and pinning Noel in her gaze. "I promise we won't tell anyone where we got the information. We have somewhat of an idea about what the program is anyway from Mark's lawyer."

Noel hesitated for a moment more before speaking. "It's software that would allow the user to take over another computer system. Countries aren't winning wars anymore based on who has the better guns or the bigger bombs. Everything now is run by computers." Noel leaned forward excitedly. "Think about it. Your electrical grid. The water supply. Every financial institution. All government entities. Everything is online or in the cloud. Everything is on some sort of computer system."

"So you're saying this program would allow the owner to take over the electrical grid?" TJ's voice was laced with the skepticism that Alexis felt. The whole thing felt more like a bad B movie than anything that could happen in real life.

Noel let out a frustrated sigh. "That's exactly what I'm saying. An electrical grid, really any system that's run by a computer, which these days is every system. Look, I know it might sound ridiculous to people not steeped in cyber warfare, but this is what I do for a living. Trust me when I say that not only is the US putting billions of dollars into developing programs like this, so are our enemies. Whoever manages to crack it first will be at a very distinct advantage."

"So how would it work?" Alexis pressed. "I mean, I know that we're always told not to click on links in emails from people we don't know. I assume the US government and whoever is in charge of our electrical and water supply has access to better protection for its computers than I have for my laptop."

"Yes and no," Noel answered. "The biggest weakness in any system is and always will be humans. No matter how much you warn them not to do something, somebody isn't going to listen. But the beauty of this program is that it doesn't matter."

Alexis felt her mouth turn down in a frown. She was getting a headache trying to keep up with Noel.

He must have noticed. "Okay, so here's an example. You remember how the federal and state governments went on hyper-alert a while back and started banning certain social media platforms on government computers that were owned by foreign companies because they worried that the foreign governments might use them to spy on Americans?"

She wasn't a regular user of social media, although she'd been telling herself for ages now that she needed to integrate it into her business model, but she vaguely remembered reading an article online on the subject. "Yeah, I think so."

She glanced at TJ, who nodded. He seemed to be having a far easier time following Noel. Maybe because of his military background, more of what Noel was saying made sense to him.

"Well, social media platforms were downloaded on millions, maybe even billions, of machines all over the world. Now imagine if simply by downloading a popular social media platform or a word processing program or any computer software, it could be infected and give a bad actor, a terrorist state, for instance, complete and total control over your computer or device. No need to wait for some clueless sap to click on a link. Nimbus attaches itself to otherwise useful code that a company pushes out to all its networked computers and bam!"

Noel clapped his hands once loudly, making Alexis jump.

"It goes to work," Noel continued excitedly. "They could see your banking information, emails, what programs you'd opened recently and all the passwords for those programs and you wouldn't even realize it. With enough computers under their control, they could harness the information and gain access to restricted servers."

"Like servers that house national security secrets, run the electrical grid..." TJ said.

Noel made a finger gun. "Exactly. Obviously, the US government would be very interested in getting its hands on a program such as this, as would many other governments."

Alexis finally felt as if she had a handle on what Noel was explaining. "And TalCon would make billions."

Noel made another finger gun and directed it at her this time.

"So that explains why someone might steal it. They could also make a lot of money selling it on the black market."

"Yes, but there is one thing," Noel said, chewing his bottom lip. "Nimbus? It doesn't work."

"It doesn't…" Alexis stuttered.

"It doesn't work. That's why I got fired. I told Bacon that we needed more time. Hell, I wasn't even one hundred percent sure we could ever make it work."

She glanced at TJ next to her, but he appeared to be just as stunned as she was.

"What did Bacon do?" TJ asked.

Noel sighed. "He went off the rails. He and Forrick had been talking up the program to the board. And I heard they'd been buzzing about it to big wigs at the Pentagon and some of the senators and representatives on various congressional committees that would have had to approve the purchase. Bacon wanted the program operational, like, yesterday, but Mark and I just couldn't make it work."

"So Mark knew the program was faulty?" TJ pressed.

Noel nodded. "He knew. He was more optimistic than I was that we could get it up and running. Eventually."

TJ frowned. "So why did you get fired but Mark didn't?"

"I confronted Bacon about hyping Nimbus to the board when he knew it wasn't going to be ready on schedule. I told him that he had an obligation to accurately report to the board, we both did, and that by not doing so we could find ourselves in a lot of hot water, not just with the board but with the SEC and other governing bodies if they felt like we were hiding the program's failures to keep the company stock from taking a hit."

"And Bacon responded by firing you," TJ summarized.

"Pretty much. There were lots of threats to go along with the firing. And blackballing. I can't get a job. People I've known and worked with in the industry for the past ten years won't return my calls. I'm starting to think I should have just kept my mouth shut like Mar—" Noel's cheeks reddened.

"Mark wouldn't have let TalCon lie to the government or the public. I'm sure he thought he had a shot at fixing the program in time."

Noel held up his hands in a surrender pose. "I'm not judging him at all. We all do what we have to do to keep food on the table. But there was no way that program was going to be ready by the end of the year like Bacon wanted."

She started to defend Mark, but TJ spoke before she could get a word out.

"So TalCon knows the program doesn't work but can't say that when they find the posting on the dark web offering it for sale so they accuse Mark of the theft, making him the fall guy?" TJ's tone said he didn't quite buy it.

"That's one possibility." Noel shot a weary glance at Alexis.

"What is it?" TJ asked while sliding his hand over hers and giving it a squeeze. She took it as a sign he knew she wasn't going to like whatever Noel was holding back.

"Look, I liked Mark. Like I said, no judgment at all. But the last couple of months we worked together, he'd been struggling."

"Struggling how?" TJ pressed.

"Drinking a lot. He never came into work out-and-out drunk," Noel added quickly. "But there were times I could smell the booze from the night before still on his breath, you know? And he'd started gambling. Ever since the MGM opened up on the National Harbor. A few of us used to go on weekends. Have a few drinks. Lose a little money. No big deal. But I think Mark got a real taste for it. He started going a lot more often than the rest of us."

Alexis's hands began to tremble.

TJ squeezed the hand he was holding just a little tighter.

"I'm sorry. I have to go." Noel pushed away from the table. "I was lucky enough to get a little freelance work and I can't afford to miss my deadlines." He stood.

TJ let go of her hand and stood as well. "Thanks for meeting with us."

Noel walked away from the table, and seconds later she heard the bell over the door ring, signaling he'd left the coffee shop.

TJ sat. "You okay?" He put an arm around her shoulder.

Alexis shook her head, looking down at the scarred table. "I'm not sure. The man Noel described was not the Mark I knew." She swallowed hard and forced herself to meet TJ's gaze. "I'm not sure I knew my brother at all."

TJ reached out and swiped at a tear that was threatening to fall. A clash of emotions rumbled through her, but desire, a hunger to feel his arms around her, pushed to the forefront.

She could see in his eyes that he was warring with the

same emotions and, more than anything, she wanted him to let go. To feel what she was feeling and to act on it.

TJ leaned forward as if he might kiss her, and she moved to meet him.

His phone rang.

He swore quietly and reached for it.

"Roman." His expression hardened a heartbeat later. He rose from the table and gestured for her to do the same, reaching out a hand.

She took it and they hurried from the café and toward the car.

Once inside, TJ switched the phone to speaker.

"It's not ideal," he said. "I'd rather meet him in person."

"He won't go for it," Shawn said on the other end of the phone. "If you want to talk to Chamberly, it's a phone call, now or never."

TJ glanced at her, and she nodded. A phone call was better than nothing. And to be honest, she was a little relieved they wouldn't have to face down the loan shark in person. Proving Mark's innocence was taking her places she'd never have imagined going. She was willing to do it for her brother, but that didn't make it any less scary.

"Okay," TJ acquiesced. "But I don't want him to know Alexis is on the line." He looked at her. "It's for your protection."

"I'm fine with that as long as I can hear the conversation," she said.

After a moment of silence, Shawn spoke again. "Chamberly, I've got TJ Roman on the line."

"Good. Fine. What is it that you want from me?" a voice with an Eastern European accent said over the line.

"Actually, I'd like to meet with you in person. I'd only take a few moments of your time."

"I'm a busy man. I don't meet with people I don't know," Chamberly said, brooking no argument. "I'm only talking to you now as a favor to a friend."

For a moment Alexis wondered just what kind of friends Shawn shared with the loan shark that made this call possible, but figured it was probably best that she didn't know the answer to that question.

"What is it you want?" Chamberly asked a second time.

Alexis got the feeling he wouldn't ask a third time.

TJ must have too. "I've been hired to look into a suspicious death of one of your clients. Mark Douglas."

"Ah, yes, Mark. I heard about his untimely passing. So sad. But he wasn't my client."

Alexis watched TJ's brow furrow. "He was seen speaking to you at the Blue Bull. That's where you do business, correct?"

There was silence on the other side of the line for a long moment. "I am part owner of the establishment."

"Listen, I don't care about your loan-sharking business," TJ said. "I'm sure that Shawn has already explained that we aren't looking to jam you up unless you had something to do with Mark Douglas's death."

"I'm not a killer. Bad for business. Mr. Douglas used to frequent my business, but our relationship ended three months ago. Amicably."

Alexis had no idea what that meant. She shot a quizzical look at TJ.

"I'm assuming that meant Mark didn't have an outstanding debt with you?"

"That's what amicable means in my business. He paid his bill with interest in March. I haven't seen him since."

Truth? Alexis mouthed at TJ.

He shrugged.

"How much did he owe you?"

Chamberly didn't answer.

"Chamberly, if you're not involved with Douglas's death, you've got nothing to worry about. You've got my word," Shawn said.

"Thirty-two thousand with interest," Chamberly finally answered.

Alexis covered her mouth just in time to stifle the gasp that escaped. Thirty-two thousand dollars? Where did Mark get that kind of money?

"Did he say where he got the money from to pay you?" TJ asked, his line of thought mirroring her own.

"No. I don't ask those kinds of questions. As long as the client has my money, I don't care where they get it from, you understand?"

"Understood. How about Nimbus? Did Mark ever mention it to you?"

"Nimbus? What is that? I've never heard of it."

"It's potentially very lucrative software. Mark never offered it to you as payment for his debts? Or maybe as security?"

Chamberly guffawed. "I'm not running a pawn shop here. This is a cash for cash operation. Douglas paid me in cold hard cash."

"Right. Thanks."

Chamberly's end of the line dropped without another word.

"You believe him?" Shawn asked.

TJ let out a heavy sigh. "Yeah. I do."

As much as Alexis wanted answers now, she had to admit she believed the loan shark, too. It didn't make sense for Chamberly to have killed Mark, and he'd seemed genuinely baffled when TJ mentioned Nimbus. Of course, it could have all been an act, but her gut was telling her that whatever happened to Mark, Chamberly didn't have anything to do with it.

"Now what?" Alexis asked. "Where do we go from here?"

Based on Shawn's silence and the look on TJ's face, neither of them were any closer to answering that question than she was.

Chapter Sixteen

TJ and Alexis returned to the safe house after meeting with Noel. Alexis went to her room, firmly closing the door behind her, a not-so-subtle hint that she wanted to be alone.

TJ settled down on the sofa with his laptop and dug deeper into Noel, TalCon, and cyber weapons generally. Noel's comments about Mark's drinking escalating and Chamberly's information about Mark's gambling problems only supported what Detective Chellel had told them. There seemed to be quite a bit about his life that Mark had been keeping a secret from his sister.

TJ felt for her. He knew it could be difficult for a family member to find out that their loved one wasn't who they thought they were. He saw it more than he liked. Wives or husbands who came to him to investigate whether their spouse was cheating or hiding money or keeping any number of secrets. Finding out that an upstanding member of the community was actually gambling away the family fortune wasn't uncommon. Neither was discovering drinking or substance abuse problems. The pressure that people found themselves under these days was often crushing, and many people turned to vices to deal with it.

Was that what had happened to Mark? Had the stress of his job, of being pressured to make Nimbus work on

TalCon's timeline, gotten to him? Had he simply snapped, figuring that if he couldn't make the program work, maybe he could still make some money off of it and when his theft was discovered he hadn't been able to deal with the fallout?

Even with everything he'd learned about his friend since starting this investigation, TJ had a hard time picturing it.

He glanced at the ceiling above, wondering how Alexis was faring with the onslaught of new information about her brother.

Even though he knew Alexis had a lot to process, it stung to have her shut him out.

But it shouldn't. She's not your girlfriend.

Definitely not. He didn't do the girlfriend thing. At least not long term. But if he did, Alexis would be exactly the kind of woman he'd want by his side.

He shook the idea from his head. He had to stop with the fantasies. He made a promise to Mark and, despite everything, he kept his promises.

The sound of footsteps overhead then on the stairs signaled Alexis's imminent arrival. But she didn't appear immediately. Instead, he heard her in the kitchen and minutes later she stepped into the living room with a steaming mug in her hand.

She sat on the sofa beside him and handed him the mug. The aroma of green tea leaves wafted under his nose.

"An apology for being so rude earlier," Alexis said, handing over the mug. "And I want to take you to lunch. Whatever you want, your choice."

"No apology necessary, but I will take you up on lunch." Without thinking, TJ set his mug aside and reached for her hand and curled his fingers through hers. "This has got to be an overwhelming situation for you. I think you're handling it as well as could be expected. Better even."

"It doesn't feel that way. I guess I needed time to process everything we just learned about Mark." Alexis dropped her head, her gaze cast down at their combined hands. "It feels like there were two Marks. The one I knew, my brother, and this other person who..." TJ saw unabated fear in her eyes and the urge to do whatever it took to banish it forever hit him like a punch in the chest. "Maybe that Mark could have done what Detective Chellel thinks he did?"

TJ used an index finger to tip her head up until her eyes met his. "Hey, we will get to the bottom of this, and whatever we find, you will get through it. I promise. And I'll be right here to help you as long as you want me."

He realized his last words could be taken more than one way.

Alexis must have heard it too. He watched an unmistakable desire flare in her eyes.

Slowly, Alexis placed a soft hand over his chest. Their gazes locked on each other.

She glided her hands up to his shoulders, leaning in.

TJ's heated gaze searched hers before his eyes fell to her mouth and she swiped her tongue over her bottom lip.

A low moan escaped from his throat, and he reached for her, closing the distance between them. He pressed his mouth to hers, his fingers kneading her back.

He tilted his head, sucking her bottom lip before deepening the kiss. She eagerly accepted him, need and desire mingling with the green tea she tasted on his lips.

Emboldened, he slipped his hands down to her backside and in one swift motion, lifted her onto his lap so she was straddling him.

She moaned as he pulled her firmly against him.

Her breasts swelled against his chest, and he imagined what it would feel like to strip her of her top and take each round bud into his mouth. His erection swelled.

Alexis broke off the kiss and met his gaze, lust swimming in her eyes. "Take me to bed."

Her words hit him like a cold shower.

He grasped her wrists gently and eased her back. "I'm sorry. I can't do this."

Confusion mixed with the lust in her eyes. "Why not?" she said, nearly breathless from his kiss.

Why not? It was a good question, one he suspected she wouldn't like his answer for.

"I'm supposed to be protecting you. Not taking advantage of you."

"You're not taking advantage. I want this, and I think you do, too."

She leaned forward, but he held her firmly. He was pretty sure he wouldn't be able to stop himself from making love to her if he let her kiss him again. "Alexis, I can't. I can't do that to Mark."

She eased off his lap. "What does Mark have to do with you and me being together?"

"You're his sister and, even though we were on the outs when he died, I still considered him my friend. My best friend. I can't do that to him. And I'm not the kind of guy you should be with anyway."

Alexis shook her head, a humorless laugh falling from her lips. "And you know the kind of guy I should be with?"

"Yes," he said, exasperated. "Someone who can give you everything you deserve. A home. Marriage. Children. I can't do any of that."

"Why not?"

"Because I don't want to." The words burst out of him now. "Because I fell in love my first year in the military. Her name was Lyssa, and I thought I'd spend my life with her. I wanted to give all of those things, but then she died and I just can't take the chance of losing someone I love again." His breaths came out in heavy puffs.

"I'm sorry you lost someone you loved, but I'm sure she wouldn't want you to cut yourself off from the possibility of ever finding someone to spend your life with. Not if she loved you as much as I can see you loved her."

On some level, he knew what Alexis said made sense, but the pain and the grief were just too deep. "I'm sorry, Alexis. I just can't."

The sorrow in her eyes mingled with pity. "I'm going to my room," she said, avoiding looking at him. "I don't think lunch is such a good idea. I've lost my appetite."

As MUCH AS he'd wanted to be with Alexis, TJ knew he'd made the right decision in stopping where they'd been headed. She deserved more than a quick roll in the hay, and he wasn't the kind of man who did relationships. The best thing he could do for her was to keep his focus on helping her find out what really happened to Mark. They'd made some progress, but there was more to do. Going to Mark's apartment to see if they could find anything there that could be of help was next on his to-do list.

He wasn't surprised when he told Alexis of his plan to search Mark's apartment that she wanted to go with him. As angry as she might have been with him, she was determined to find the answers to the questions surrounding her brother's death. She didn't say a single word to him on the drive to the apartment, however. She wouldn't even look at him. It felt like his insides were being scooped out with a spoon, but he knew it was for the best. He had to nip the feelings building between them in the bud now before they got out of hand. As much as he wanted to kiss her and more, he couldn't change who he was.

A man who was afraid of getting his heart broken again.

Mark had rented one side of a duplex in suburban Alexandria. The duplex's owner, Mark's landlord, occupied the other side. The small yard in front of the home was well taken care of, neatly cut grass edged with a flower bed blooming with brightly colored tulips. The driveway looked as if someone had recently touched up the asphalt, and the detached garage TJ glimpsed from the front of the house looked to have been recently painted.

There was no car in the shared driveway when TJ parked at the curb and no one answered the landlord's door when he and Alexis knocked to let the man know they'd be clearing out some of Mark's things today.

Alexis's hand shook as she stuck the key into the lock on the door.

"You okay?" TJ gazed down at her. He was more than a little emotional himself. He couldn't imagine what Alexis was feeling at the moment.

But she nodded. "Yeah. It's time I do this. Mark's landlord has contacted me about getting his things. Knowing what I know now about Mark being late on the rent so much, he's actually been rather kind in not pushing me to clear out the place sooner."

They'd stopped and picked up several boxes and some packing tape on the way to Mark's house. Alexis had been all in on focusing on packing up Mark's things rather than the information Detective Chellel and Noel Muscarelli had told them about Mark, but packing up her dead brother's things seemed to be hitting her hard now.

The small one-bedroom space was clean and functional. A long black leather sofa with colorful throw pillows faced a large wall-mounted flat-screen television and a glass-top coffee table. Two end tables, each with a porcelain lamp, flanked the sofa. A flowery tablecloth covered the dining table that separated the living room from the kitchen. Frilly curtains hung at the single large window in the living room.

"This place is freezing," Alexis said, turning up the thermostat on the wall.

She wasn't wrong about that, but still a musty odor hung in the air. TJ recognized it as the smell of a space that had sat uninhabited for too long.

"We'll warm up as we work," he said, although he elected to keep his coat on for the time being.

Alexis appeared to have the same idea, pulling the zipper on the padded vest she wore over her thick sweater higher as she ambled to the opposite side of the living room. Keeping her distance. He fought the internal push-pull of wanting her close but needing to hold her at arm's length.

"Is there somewhere you want to start?" he asked, focusing back on the task at hand.

They weren't just there to pack up Mark's things. The Mark that he and Alexis knew and the Mark that Detective Chellel and Noel Muscarelli described were so different, TJ hoped that he'd find something in his old friend's apartment that would help traverse the gulf between the two Marks. Something that would help stem the turmoil he felt. He didn't want to believe that Mark could have done what he was accused of, but Detective Chellel wasn't wrong about financial stress and substance abuse making people do things that they wouldn't otherwise do. If Mark was really in as much financial trouble as Detective Chellel said he was, maybe he'd seen stealing Nimbus as his only way out.

He knew that Alexis would never believe her brother was a thief, though. Not without irrefutable proof.

"Why don't you start by packing up Mark's clothes? I'm sure Mark wouldn't like his sister rooting around in his underwear drawer," Alexis said without looking at him. "I'll pack up the kitchen."

"Okay," TJ answered, hesitant to leave her in the room alone, although he figured that was exactly why she'd made the suggestion. "Remember to be on the lookout for anything that might help the investigation. Papers. Notes. Journals. A flash drive."

Alexis frowned, but nodded.

TJ headed into Mark's room. A mattress and box spring sat on a metal frame, no headboard, with a blue comforter and another bunch of throw pillows covering it. The same frilly curtains from the living room hung on the window in the bedroom.

The closet door stood open. Although Mark may have lived simply in most respects, TJ wasn't surprised to see the closet packed full of clothes. Clothes had always been one area where Mark liked to indulge. His favorite saying was "the clothes make the man."

"Alexis, you should see this," he called, moving over to the nightstand beside the bed.

He picked up a framed photo and turned as Alexis entered the room.

"What is it?"

TJ nodded at the photo in his hand. "Didn't you say Mark and Jessica broke up? Why would he keep her photo by the bed?"

Her hand brushed against his as he handed the photo to her. A charge of desire sparked in him. He met her gaze and found desire that matched his own there. Despite everything he'd said earlier, the attraction between them was undeniable. If she was anyone other than Mark's sister...

Alexis stepped back, taking the photo with her, and looked down at it. When she looked at him again, the moment had passed.

"I don't know," she said. "If she and Mark were still together, where is she? She wasn't at his funeral, and I haven't heard from her."

"That's a good question and one we'll definitely want—"

TJ was interrupted by the sound of glass shattering in the living room, followed by a thundering whoosh.

He ran out into the hall.

Fire raced up the curtains and along the cheap carpeting covering the floor. The gaping hole in the window was evidence of the fire's origin. Someone had thrown a Molotov cocktail through the window.

The sound of more glass shattering and a crash sent him racing back into Mark's bedroom.

A second firebomb had come through the bedroom window, landing on the bed and engulfing it in flames.

Alexis crouched on the floor near the closet, her hands covering her head.

"Alexis! Are you okay?"

She looked up at him from her crouched position. "I ducked," she said, her voice shaky. "It…it just missed me."

"We have to get out of here."

He helped her to her feet.

Thick smoke filled the apartment.

"Cover your mouth," TJ ordered, shielding his own mouth as best he could, using the sleeve of his shirt.

Alexis did the same, and together they made their way into the hallway.

The living room was nearly completely engulfed in flames now. There was no way they could reach the front door without going through the fire.

"Does this place have a rear entrance?" TJ asked, casting about for another means of getting out.

Alexis coughed. "No."

TJ glanced back at the bedroom. The window in the room was big enough for them to get out of, but the fire had totally engulfed the bed and it was far closer to the window than he would have liked when making an escape.

There was only one other possibility.

"In here."

TJ pulled Alexis into the bathroom and shut the door behind them. He grabbed one of the two towels from the towel rack on the wall and stuffed it under the door. He wet the second towel and handed it to Alexis. "Use that to cover your face."

"What about you?" Alexis asked, doing as he told her.

TJ studied the window above the bathroom sink. "I'm going to work on getting us out of here."

He hopped up on the countertop and flicked the latch on the window. It opened, but when he tried pulling the windowpane open, it wouldn't budge. It had been painted over at some point.

He had to get that window open. Hopefully, a neighbor or a passerby had already seen the smoke and flames and called the fire department, but he couldn't wait around. The fire was consuming the duplex, and he and Alexis might not have much more time before the smoke overwhelmed them. The window was their only path to safety.

He jumped off the counter and scanned the bathroom. There wasn't much that looked like it could be of any use, but maybe if he could get the towel rod off the wall.

He grabbed the towel rod and yanked. Catching onto his plan, Alexis joined him, pulling on the other end.

It took longer than he'd have liked under the circumstances, but the rod finally came away from the wall.

"Stand back," he ordered Alexis, hopping back up on the counter with the rod in his hand.

He slammed the rod into the window, shattering the glass. A few more strikes and all the glass gave way.

"Okay," he said, hopping down off the counter again. "Up you go and through the window."

Alexis gave the small opening the once-over. "I'm not sure I'll fit."

TJ placed a hand on either of her shoulders and looked her in the eye. "It's our only way out, so you'll have to."

He steadied her as she climbed on the counter. She stuck her head out of the opening, wiggling until her entire torso was out.

"I don't think I'm going to make it." Her voice floated back through the window.

TJ hopped onto the counter again and placed his hands

on her bottom. "On the count of three, I'm going to push. One. Two. Three."

He shoved, and Alexis tumbled the rest of the way out of the window. He had nearly as much trouble getting out of the small window, but he finally managed to squeeze his body through.

TJ crawled away from the house toward where Alexis lay on the grass in the backyard.

"Are you okay?" he asked, scanning her body. There were visible cuts and bruises on her hands.

"I think...my arm." She clutched her right forearm.

Her vest was covered in soot, not unlike his own clothing. But it was the lower portion of her right sleeve that he noticed now. It was burned away and her usually smooth brown skin was red and raw. The second Molotov cocktail hadn't missed her after all. It must have caught the sleeve of her shirt. It was a miracle that it hadn't done more damage.

TJ swore, which led to a coughing fit. He patted his back pocket where his cell phone should be and found that it was missing. He'd probably dropped it in the chaos of trying to get out of the fire.

Luckily, he could hear sirens approaching.

Alexis groaned next to him.

He gathered her in his arms. "It's okay, baby. It's alright. Help will be here any second now."

Help was on the way, and as soon as he was sure that Alexis would be okay, he was going to find the bastard who had just tried to kill them and make him pay.

Chapter Seventeen

TJ paced the hospital waiting room.

The EMTs had allowed him to ride in the ambulance with Alexis but the nurses wouldn't let him go any further than the emergency room waiting area. That had been more than an hour earlier, and no one was giving him any information about Alexis's condition. He was getting desperate.

Alexis's burns had looked serious.

He should have moved faster. Been paying more attention to whether or not they were being followed. All his bravado from the hours before was gone, leaving nothing but guilt and regret for having taken on a case he was utterly unqualified to handle.

He'd spent the last hour beating himself up for not having anticipated the second firebomb. It galled him to admit it, but the truth was that he was in way over his head. The most important thing to him was that Alexis be kept safe, and he knew now that he wasn't the man who could make that happen. As soon as he was sure Alexis was okay, he was going to turn her case over to Shawn or another West operative with more experience in dangerous, complex cases.

The doors to the ER opened and Detective Chellel strode into the waiting room.

"Roman! What the hell have you and Miss Douglas gotten yourselves into?"

"We haven't gotten ourselves into anything," TJ responded, facing the detective down. "Someone tried to kill us."

"You had no business being at Mark Douglas's place. The arson inspector tells me the entire space is a loss."

"Alexis had every right to be there. It's her brother's place, and we were there packing up his things."

"Right," Chellel scoffed. "Packing. And snooping, no doubt. You don't think we scoured every inch of that place before we released it?"

TJ fisted his hands on his hips. "Well, then you don't have to worry. We'll find anything you missed."

Detective Chellel let out a long, slow breath. "I'm not here to fight with you. How is Miss Douglas?"

TJ ran a shaky hand over his head. "I don't know. No one has told me anything since they took her in the back. Her arm was burned pretty badly."

"She's tough. I know that for a fact. She'll be okay."

Alexis was tough, but that did nothing to keep him from worrying about her.

"The officer who took your statements at the scene gave me a brief rundown on what happened, but I'd like to hear the details from you if I could."

The detective led him to a bank of chairs, and they sat.

"We went to Mark's place to pack up some of his things, but also to look around, see if we could find anything that might point toward someone other than Mark as the thief."

"And did you find anything?"

"We weren't in the apartment long enough to find anything before the first firebomb came through the window."

Detective Chellel pulled a small notebook from her purse. "And that was the one that was thrown into the living room, correct?"

"Yes, a Molotov cocktail came through the living room window and about thirty seconds later, a second bomb was thrown through the bedroom window."

Detective Chellel took notes. "And you and Miss Douglas didn't see anyone before the fire broke out. No movement outside the windows? The sounds of someone prowling around outside?"

"No. Nothing, but I was…distracted," he conceded.

"Distracted?" Chellel gave him a knowing look.

There was no way he was going to confirm what she appeared to be thinking, so he told a half truth. "I'd just found a photo of Mark's ex-girlfriend next to his bed. Alexis believed that Mark and Jessica had broken up, so we were surprised to see the photo."

Detective Chellel flipped back several pages in her notebook. "Jessica Castaldo. I spoke to her. She said that she and Mark had an on-again, off-again relationship that was off when he died."

TJ arched his brow. "Are you sure Mark knew that? It would be strange for him to have kept a photo of a woman who wasn't his girlfriend next to his bed."

Chellel looked thoughtful. "I'll have another chat with her, but I'm not sure it relates to the attack on you and Miss Douglas today."

Detective Chellel was stubborn. But so was he. "This is your case too?"

"Someone burns down the house of my suspect in a major theft. Yeah, it's my case."

"At least you acknowledge it's related," TJ mumbled.

"Look, Mr. Roman, I know you and Miss Douglas don't think much of my investigative skills, but I know my job and I'm good at it. I told you earlier that I've always had my suspicions that Mark Douglas had an accomplice. The attacks on you and Miss Douglas support that theory."

TJ shook his head. "But you still think Mark was involved?"

"The evidence is the evidence."

The doors to the waiting room slid open again. A woman in blue scrubs with a surgical mask dangling from one ear stepped into the room, her eyes scanning the seats. "Mr. Roman?"

"Here." TJ raised his hand as if he was in school, his heart rate picking up speed.

"Miss Douglas is asking for you. If you'll follow me."

TJ looked at the detective.

"Go ahead." She waved him away. "I know where to find you if I have any more questions."

He followed the nurse down a long, bright hallway until they reached a curtained-off section. The nurse pulled the curtain back.

His breath caught in his chest when he saw her. Alexis reclined on the bed, her eyes closed. She wore a hospital gown and the lower part of her right arm was heavily bandaged.

She opened her eyes as he made his way to her bedside. "Hi."

"Hi, you. How are you feeling?"

"A little groggy. They gave me the good stuff to take the edge off."

He took the hand on her unbandaged arm and pressed a kiss to her knuckles. "I'm so sorry."

She reached up and ran her hand over his jaw. "You have nothing to be sorry for. You didn't set Mark's place on fire."

"I should have been paying more attention. I should have anticipated the second Molotov cocktail."

"You can't blame yourself."

Maybe she didn't blame him, but he could definitely blame himself.

"I'm going to turn the case over to Shawn. I don't know what I'm doing and I'd never forgive myself if something happened to you because of that. Mark would never forgive me."

"No." Alexis struggled to get into a more upright position.

"Hey, hey, take it easy." He helped her sit up.

"Listen to me. I need you. Not Shawn West or anyone else. I need you to do this. You knew Mark and loved him as much as I did, but you also saw the flaws that I couldn't. I trust you to tell me if my love for him is getting in the way of my objectivity. No one else can do that."

The nurse who'd brought him to Alexis appeared around the curtain. "I'm sorry. Miss Douglas needs to rest. The doctor is going to keep her overnight. You can come back tomorrow."

Alexis gripped his arm. "Please, TJ. Think about what I said. I need you."

He bent and pressed a featherlight kiss to her lips.

He'd think about what she'd asked of him. But he'd do what he thought was best.

TJ WAS TORN. Alexis had been discharged from the hospital the next morning. He'd gotten her settled at the safe house then made a quick run to the grocery store, loading up on food for them with the intention on staying in for the next day or two so she could rest and heal.

He hadn't stopped thinking about what she'd said about needing him to stay on the case. After a lot of back and forth with himself, he'd decided to stick it out on the condition that she spend the morning resting, which she had. But as morning changed to early afternoon, Alexis began to push for them to get back to investigating.

He thought the best thing for her would be to stay in bed and rest. But he also didn't want to waste any more time before speaking to Lenora Kenda. Still, he didn't feel comfortable leaving Alexis alone. Not that it seemed to matter. Alexis made it clear that the decision wasn't his to make. She'd insisted that she was fine and that she couldn't take any more rest. They'd spent some time compiling as much information as possible on Lenora Kenda and planning how they'd go about interviewing her since she was clearly avoiding them. They settled on an unannounced visit to her home and figured since she was a mom, the best time to catch her would be around dinnertime.

Lenora Kenda lived in a modest craftsman-style home in a middle-class neighborhood. The background search he'd done on Mark's assistant revealed that she was a single mother of two. That made the extended vacation Nelson Bacon had said she'd taken more than a little suspect to TJ's mind. Single mothers tended to save their vacation days for things like sick kids, snow days off of school, and other unexpected kid-related events. Based on the lights blazing in the windows of the house, Lenora was taking a staycation.

TJ climbed out of the car and rounded the hood to the passenger side. He scanned the street, looking for signs of anyone who didn't belong. He'd been equally vigilant on the drive to the Kenda home, twisting through less-traveled residential streets to make sure they weren't being followed. He hadn't seen anyone, but given the lengths Alexis's pursuers had already gone through to get to her, he wasn't under any illusions that they'd stop until she dropped her investigation. Since Alexis had made it clear that she had no intention of doing that, he had to step up his game and do everything he could to protect her.

He helped Alexis out of the car and they climbed the stairs onto the wide porch that wrapped around the front of the Kenda home. TJ rang the doorbell, and he and Alexis waited more than a minute before the curtain on the side window was pulled back. A blonde woman with a bob haircut and the same green eyes TJ had seen in the photo that had been in the background report on Lenora Kenda peered out at them.

"Can I help you?" Lenora asked, suspicion ringing in her voice. She was wearing a blue cardigan over a white shirt, black pants and well-worn slippers.

"Ms. Kenda? My name is Alexis Douglas. Mark was my brother. I was hoping I could ask you a few questions."

"Who is he?" Lenora said. Her skittish gaze shifted from Alexis to TJ and back again.

"This is TJ Roman." Alexis gestured toward him. "He's a friend, and he also knew my brother. He's helping me sort out the events leading up to Mark's death. I'm hoping you can help us."

Lenora disappeared from the window. Seconds later, the door opened a crack. "I already talked to the police."

"I know," Alexis said, "but I'm not sure the police are on the right track."

Lenora glanced back inside the house nervously. "It's a school night and the kids have homework." She started to close the door.

Alexis put out a hand, stopping the door from closing. "Please. Mark always spoke highly of you. This will only take a few minutes."

Lenora hesitated for several moments longer. "Okay, but just for a few minutes." She moved aside so they could step inside. The house had a warm, cozy, lived-in feel. Shoes lined the wall by the door and a table next to the stairs was littered with unopened mail, keys and a black leather purse. A formal dining room was to the right of the front door, and TJ could see the kitchen down a hall at the rear of the house. Classical music floated from the back of the house.

A preteen girl with blonde hair the same shade as Lenora's but that hung down past her shoulders stepped out of the kitchen. "Mom?"

"It's okay, sweetheart. These people just want to ask me some questions about my boss."

The preteen let out a put-upon sigh. "The police again? What was this guy, some kind of uber-criminal?"

"Annie, please. Go finish up dinner with your sister and then help her get started on her homework."

Annie sighed again but flounced back into the kitchen.

"Sorry about that." Lenora led them into the living room. "Whoever said the terrible twos are the worst should wait until those toddlers become preteens."

The room was dominated by a large blue sectional that faced an entertainment system. The walls held framed family photos starting with Lenora, with a man TJ assumed was her husband and a baby who must have been Annie. The photos progressed to show a family of four. Lenora's background report showed that she'd divorced her husband five years earlier. The most recent photos showed Lenora flanked by her two girls alone.

Lenora gestured toward the comfortable sectional.

TJ took a seat next to Alexis on one end and Lenora sat on the other end.

"You're a difficult woman to get a hold of," TJ began.

Lenora shifted nervously on the sofa. "Yes, well, I am sorry about not returning your calls. With work and the girls, I get very busy at times."

"We spoke with Nelson Bacon and Arnold Forrick and they said you were taking some vacation time."

"I… I needed time. Mark's death is a lot to process. I'm sure you two of all people understand being his sister and friend."

"It has been a difficult time. That's why I'm here. Trying to make sense of it. Ms. Kenda—"

"Please, you can call me Lenora."

"Lenora." Alexis smiled. "I don't think Mark stole anything and there's no way he committed suicide."

Lenora shook her head. "I only know what the police told me."

"Did you notice anything strange or out of the ordinary in the days or weeks before the theft?" TJ asked. They needed details, specifics that could lead them to the person who had Nimbus now and who had most likely attacked them.

"No. Nothing." Lenora's gaze skipped away to the wall of photos.

"You're lying," TJ barked, sending Lenora jumping in her seat.

He might have gone easier on Mark's assistant if she

hadn't been avoiding speaking to them. It was obvious the woman knew more than what she was saying, and he was losing his patience.

"I'm not. I don't know anything."

Alexis scooted forward on the sofa. "You worked with my brother every day for more than five years. You spent more time with him than I did. Do you think he stole the Nimbus program from TalCon with the intention of selling it on the black market?"

Lenora clenched her hands together. "The police say—"

"I know what the police are saying. I want to know what you think."

Torment flashed across Lenora's face. "I have children."

"Is someone threatening you?" TJ asked.

Lenora nodded.

TJ softened his tone. "Lenora, we will keep you safe. I promise you, but we need to know what you know."

A tear slid down Lenora's face, and her hands shook. "I didn't know what I was seeing."

Alexis covered the woman's hands with her own. "What did you see?"

"One night several months ago, I left my cell phone at the office. It was a Friday night, and the girls were going to have a sleepover at a friend's house. After I dropped them off, I went back to the office to get my phone."

TJ wanted to hurry her along but knew it would be counterproductive, so he dipped into his storeroom of patience.

"I saw a man in Mark's office at his computer," she answered softly.

"Did you recognize him?"

"No. I didn't know him, but when I asked what he was doing, he said he was from the IT department and that he was just installing some updates to the computer," she said, her eyes darting around the room evasively.

"But you were suspicious," Alexis said.

"He looked the part, button-down shirt, khakis, wire-rimmed glasses. Even had a pocket protector in his shirt pocket. But it just felt like something wasn't right, you know? I'm not very computer savvy, so I've interacted with most of the people in IT at some point or another. So there was no reason for me to think much of it…"

"Until…" TJ pressed. Lenora's body language screamed that there was something she was holding back.

"The next day I took myself out for brunch before I had to pick up the girls. The man from Mark's office sat down at my table. The IT nerd was long gone. He was in all black and he looked…scary. He asked if I'd told anyone I'd seen him that night in Mark's office, and when I said no, he said if I told anyone, my daughters would have a very bad accident. He threatened my daughters. And then after Mark was accused of stealing the program, the man came back."

"You saw him a third time?"

"He came to my house. With Annie." Lenora's shoulders shook from crying now. "She'd biked to her friend's house and the chain had broken on the way back. He offered her a ride and thank God she knew better than to get in the car with a strange man, but she didn't see any harm when he offered to walk with her to make sure she got home safe. It was only a few blocks but…"

TJ knew the distance wasn't the point. Terror was. A mother's children were always her soft spot. "He wanted to make sure you knew he could get to you and the girls."

Lenora glanced over her shoulder toward the back of the house. They could hear the girls talking in the kitchen.

"He reminded me not to do anything foolish. That I had better keep my mouth shut."

"And you did," Alexis said. "You didn't tell Detective Chellel any of this?"

"No. I... I couldn't risk it." Lenora collapsed her hands together in a death grip.

"Not even when Mark was under suspicion? When he died and the police called it a suicide?"

Lenora met Alexis's angry gaze with a direct one of her own. "You don't have any children, do you? I'm sorry about Mark, but I don't know if the accusations against him are true or not. Even if I did, you can't expect me to risk my children."

Alexis scowled. "Is that why you've been on an extended vacation?"

"Yes. I don't know who the man is or how he got into TalCon, but I don't feel safe there anymore. I'm pretty sure I'm going to look for a new job, but the company is being very generous, allowing me to take as much time off as I need in light of Mark's death."

"Mom?" Annie poked her head around the corner of the wall. "Are you okay?"

Lenora wiped her eyes. "I'm fine, honey. Just a little sad about my boss. Remember, I told you he passed away. This is his sister."

"Yeah, ah, I'm sorry about your brother." Annie shifted from one foot to the other.

"We'll be through here in just a minute. If you've finished your homework, you can have a little TV time."

Annie hesitated for a long moment, unsure if she should leave her mother before disappearing back into the kitchen.

"We just need a few more minutes of your time. Can you describe the man who threatened you?" TJ asked.

"Um…he was tall, over six feet. White guy with dark hair."

"Any distinguishing marks? Maybe a tattoo?"

Lenora nodded. "He had a tattoo on his neck. A coiled snake ready to strike." A small shiver stole through her body.

"Lenora, this is really important. I need you to think back. What day, exactly, was it that you saw this man in Mark's office?"

Lenora squeezed her hands together tighter still and looked at them woefully. TJ knew what she was going to say before she said it. "It was exactly one week before Mark was accused of stealing the program."

Chapter Eighteen

Alexis insisted on heading to the police station to share the information that Lenora Kenda had given them with Detective Chellel. It felt like they had finally gotten a break that might help them prove Mark's innocence, but TJ seemed almost reticent about the turn in their investigation.

"Hey, this is great news. Why aren't you happier about it?"

"I am happy. Lenora's statement gives Detective Chellel someone to look at for the theft other than Mark and that is great."

"So why the frowny face? What are you thinking?"

"There was something she wasn't telling us. It was something in her body language. She wouldn't look either of us in the eye when she answered certain questions, and she was so nervous."

"Maybe," Alexis said, recalling Lenora's actions as she answered their questions. "But with the threats that guy made against her and her kids, she had reason to be scared. That could be all it was."

"It's possible."

But Alexis could tell TJ didn't think fear was all it was. If Lenora knew more, they could get it out of her later. For now, they had a place to start with the information she had given them.

The detective had dismissed Alexis's assertions that Mark couldn't be the thief before, but now Detective Chellel would have to take her seriously. Lenora's statement proved that someone other than Mark had been at this computer station at the time the Nimbus program was downloaded.

Once again, they gave their names to the clerk at the reception desk. TJ's phone beeped with an incoming text while they were waiting for an escort to take them back to meet with Detective Chellel.

"What is it?" Alexis asked.

"Shawn," he answered his eyes still on the phone. "He got an address for Jessica."

The heavy doors leading beyond the station's reception area opened and a uniformed cop barked at them to follow him to the conference room. Detective Chellel was already waiting for them when they arrived.

"Miss Douglas." Detective Chellel rose from her seat at the table when TJ and Alexis entered. "I was just about to contact you."

"Detective, we have new information for you. TJ and I have just come from speaking to Lenora Kenda."

Detective Chellel looked surprised. "Mark Douglas's assistant."

"The very one," TJ said.

"Sit." Detective Chellel waved them toward chairs.

Alexis ignored her. She was too excited to sit. "Lenora Kenda saw someone, not Mark, at Mark's desk, on his computer on the night the Nimbus program had been illegally downloaded. She described the man to us."

TJ broke in then, relaying to Detective Chellel the concise description that they'd gotten from Lenora.

Detective Chellel frowned. "Hang on a minute. What were you two doing talking to Lenora Kenda?"

Alexis fisted her hands on her hips. "We were doing what you couldn't or wouldn't. Looking for the truth about what happened to my brother."

Detective Chellel let out a breath that was half sigh, half growl. "Ms. Douglas—"

"May I suggest," TJ spoke up, "that you listen to what we have to say first? Then you can dress us down however you'd like."

Detective Chellel's eyes narrowed in on TJ, her frown deepening into a scowl. "Fine. Tell me what you know," she said finally.

"On the night Mark supposedly stole Nimbus, Lenora Kenda saw a man she didn't recognize working at his computer. She'd gone back to the office because she'd forgotten her cell phone. She said the man said he was upgrading the computer system, but she found the situation suspicious."

"If she found this man suspicious, why didn't she say something when I questioned her after the theft or after your brother's death?"

"She was scared," TJ said. "She said that the day after she saw the man, he showed up at the restaurant where she was having brunch and threatened her children if she told anyone what she saw."

Detective Chellel swore. "I need to speak to her again."

"You need to look for this man she saw. He's the one who stole Nimbus, and he probably killed my brother."

Detective Chellel sighed heavily. "I will follow up with Ms. Kenda." She gestured again toward a chair. "Ms. Douglas, please sit down. There is something I need to speak with you about."

Alexis had expected more of a fight to get Detective Chellel to listen. The detective giving in so easily sent a shot of nerves through her. She caught a look from TJ. He also seemed to sense something was up.

She swayed on her feet. TJ's arm wrapped around her waist and he guided her into a seat before sitting in the chair next to her.

Detective Chellel opened a manila folder Alexis hadn't noticed lying on the table. The detective scanned the top sheet of what appeared to be several sheets stapled together before looking up at them again. "We got the complete toxicology report back. There was diazepam in your brother's system, but not enough to kill him. It appears the undigested pills he took were the only pills ingested."

Alexis's mind churned in confusion. "What does that mean?"

"It means someone wanted us to think Mark overdosed on Valium. They might have forced him to take a few pills, or maybe they just waited until he'd taken them himself. But that wasn't what killed him. The toxicology report showed that Mark had over fifteen hundred micrograms of fentanyl in his system."

Alexis's stomach dropped to her toes. She felt TJ's hand wrap around hers and hold on tight.

"No! Mark was a drinker, sometimes a heavy one, yes, but he'd never use drugs."

"We know," Detective Chellel said. "We don't think your brother introduced the fentanyl into his system voluntarily. Since the medical examiner is sure there were no injection marks on Mark's body, we believe the drug was introduced orally or nasally when your brother was unconscious." Detective Chellel closed her file. "I'm very sorry."

Hot tears rolled down Alexis's cheeks. She glared at Detective Chellel. "I told you Mark wouldn't have committed suicide."

"I had to follow the evidence." Chellel had the grace to look away from Alexis as she spoke. "Just like I will do now. I will follow up with Ms. Kenda and on the information we've obtained from this report to see if I can trace where these drugs came from. We know the diazepam was prescribed by Mark's primary care physician. Do you have any idea who would know he was taking the drug?"

"No." Alexis wiped at her eyes. "I mean, he didn't even tell me he was on medication. Maybe his on-again, off-again girlfriend Jessica?"

Detective Chellel shook her head. "She said she didn't know about the diazepam. Of course, I'll be talking to her again."

"Maybe Lenora Kenda," TJ offered. "In my experience, secretaries and assistants typically know more about the people they work for than those people think."

Detective Chellel's brow rose to her hairline. "You have a point there. I'll ask her about it."

"What's next?" Alexis asked Detective Chellel.

"Next, I will continue to do my job and investigate this case." The detective's answer was pointed. "You and Mr. Roman have been a big help." The detective struggled to get that last sentence out. "But as you are quite aware, this case is proving dangerous. We have someone out there who isn't afraid of killing people in order to sell this Nimbus program. You two need to back off. Leave this to law enforcement to handle."

Alexis almost responded that if she and TJ hadn't started their own investigation, Detective Chellel and her department would be even further behind in their investigation of Mark's death than they currently were. The detective had wasted weeks investigating the case as a suicide as a result of the theft. Who knew what evidence had been lost in those weeks?

TJ squeezed her hand and Alexis took it as a sign she shouldn't say what she'd been thinking. She stayed silent.

"Thank you for keeping us updated on the case," TJ said, standing as if ready to leave. "I hope we can count on you to continue to keep us in the loop as the case progresses."

Alexis rose along with Detective Chellel.

"I'll do what I can." The detective's tone was noncommittal.

Alexis and TJ said their goodbyes to the detective and made their way back to the parking garage.

Inside the car, Alexis broke down.

TJ held her close, whispering in her ear that everything would be okay until the storm of emotion passed.

After several minutes, she slid out of his arms. "Sorry. It's just, I knew my brother would never kill himself and when Detective Chellel finally said she believed that too…"

"You have nothing to feel sorry for. With everything you've been through in the last several weeks… I'm amazed at your strength."

TJ started the SUV and pointed them toward the safe house.

"Are you going to do what the detective said and leave the investigating to the cops now?" he asked after several minutes of driving in silence.

"No way," Alexis scoffed. "I'm hopeful that the detective will have a more open mind now that she knows for a fact that Mark was murdered, but she's bungled this investigation from the beginning. I'm not ready to put my faith in her now."

"Me either. So you're thinking what I'm thinking then. We keep moving forward in our own investigation."

Alexis gazed up at her brother's best friend and the man she'd fallen hard for. "I'm not stopping until Mark's name is completely cleared and we prove he was murdered."

"So, WHAT'S OUR next step?" Alexis asked.

"Our conversation with Detective Chellel reminded me that we still need to talk to Jessica Castaldo. I say we drop in on her and see what she can tell us."

"Sounds good."

"Her address is on my phone." TJ jerked his head toward his phone in the cup holder in the center console. "Could you get it for me?" He gave Alexis his password, and she checked it out on the screen. A moment later, they had the address plugged into the phone's GPS system and were on their way.

"It feels like we're finally making some progress at least," Alexis said soberly. "I know Detective Chellel doesn't believe Mark wasn't involved in the theft yet, but now that we know he didn't kill himself..." The rest of what she was about to say was swallowed by a sob.

TJ reached across the console and took her hand in his, squeezing it. "Hey, take a breath. You've been dealing with a lot. Should I pull over?"

With her free hand, she swiped at the tears falling from her eyes. "No, no. We need to talk to Jessica and I don't want to waste any more time. It just finally hit me that if Mark didn't commit suicide, that means he was murdered."

TJ had wondered when that revelation would finally

sink in, and now that it had, he felt she was strong enough to deal with it. He would help her any way he could.

He glanced in the rearview mirror and spotted a large black SUV speeding toward them. He changed lanes, but the SUV changed lanes with him.

TJ pressed down on the accelerator and the car moved forward faster.

"What's wrong?" Alexis asked, fear edging her words.

"We're being followed. The black SUV behind us has been following for the last several miles."

Alexis twisted in her seat so she could get a look at the car through the rearview window. She reported that the driver was male with dark hair, but the glare from the sun kept her from seeing much more detail.

The SUV behind them sped up and rammed into their car. TJ fought to keep their rental on the road and avoid hitting the car in the lane next to them. He stomped down on the accelerator and the car lurched forward.

"He's crazy. He's gonna get us killed."

"I think that's his plan," TJ said, keeping his eyes on the road in front of him.

The SUV hit their car again, sending the rental skidding across the road. Thankfully, there was not another car next to them, but that didn't stop the horns from the surrounding cars from blaring. Hopefully, one of the other drivers was calling the police and getting help. But until help arrived, they were going to have to try to outrun the SUV.

The SUV slammed into the back of the sedan a third time. This time the car spun, clipping the rear bumper of a pickup truck before TJ got control of the car again. Unfortunately, they were facing the wrong way on the highway.

Car horns blared as the other drivers swerved to avoid

hitting them. TJ punched the car forward and turned the wheel so that they did a 180-degree turn and faced the right way again. The engine roared as he raced down the pavement and attempted to get away from the SUV.

"Can you reach your phone?" TJ asked. "Call for help."

Alexis reached toward the passenger floor for her purse between her feet, but before she could grab it, the SUV hit them again and she lurched forward, barely managing to keep her chest from slamming against the dashboard.

A loud pop ricocheted around the interior of the car.

"What was that?" Alexis exclaimed in a voice laden with panic.

TJ's gaze went to the rearview mirror, and he swore. "He's shooting at us."

Another round of gunshots sounded, joining the cacophony of car horns from the other drivers on the road.

Another loud pop and the back of the car fishtailed.

"He shot out our tire," TJ yelled, fighting to regain control of the car, to no avail.

They clipped the side of a BMW, and then they were tumbling. Over and over until the car came to a stop on its roof, the passenger side door smashed against the side of an old oak tree.

TJ groaned and turned his head slowly to look at her. "Alexis, are you OK? Baby, are you hurt?"

She seemed to take stock of her body. "I'm OK. How about you?"

There was an angry red scratch just above TJ's eyebrow. "I'm fine. But my seat belt is jammed."

Alexis pressed the release button on her seat belt, but it would not give. "My belt is stuck too." She looked up from the belt and gasped. "TJ, he's coming." She pointed at the driver's side window.

The driver from the SUV, clad in all black, marched toward them with a silver pistol in his right hand. "We have to get out of here!"

She pressed frantically at the seat belt release, but the buckle held fast.

TJ tried reaching for his ankle. "I can't reach my gun."

Suddenly, the man stopped and glanced over his shoulder. It took a moment before TJ realized why, but then the sound of sirens reached his ears. The SUV driver looked back at them, pure venom in his eyes, before spinning around and running back toward the highway.

Alexis let out a breath.

"He's gone," TJ said.

The sound of the sirens grew closer until they were almost deafening. They could see red and blue swirls at the top of the incline that led back to the highway.

"He's gone, but I recognized him, TJ."

"You recognized him?"

"Yes. That was the man who killed my brother."

Chapter Nineteen

Two police cruisers and an ambulance crowded the break-down lane that ran along the side of the highway. The sun had already fallen below the horizon, leaving the sky a dusky blue color. A tow truck had arrived only moments earlier to pull their rental car out of the ditch, limiting the drivers on the road to a single lane. The traffic passed by slowly, the drivers shooting curious glances at the commotion on the side of the road.

TJ and Alexis sat between the open back doors of the ambulance. TJ had a gash along his right shoulder from where his seat belt had dug into his skin. The EMTs wanted him to go to the hospital to get it stitched up, but he declined. He'd had far worse injuries and, at the moment, he had bigger issues to attend to than a gash on his shoulder.

He wasn't surprised when a black, unmarked police car screeched to a stop behind the ambulance and Detective Chellel sprung from the car.

"What the hell have you two gotten yourselves into now?" Detective Chellel demanded.

Alexis frowned. "We're both fine, Detective. Thanks for your concern."

"Why should I be concerned for your safety when clearly

neither of you are," the detective growled. "Now, what's going on here?"

"We were forced off the road," TJ said.

"And shot at," Alexis added.

"Did you get a good look at your assailant?" the detective asked.

"I can tell you he drove a black SUV with no license plates." TJ waved away the EMT, who was still fussing with the scratch on his shoulder and shrugged back into his coat.

Alexis stood. "It was the same guy Lenora Kenda saw in Mark's office. The same guy who threatened her."

"How can you be sure of that?" Detective Chellel's tone was infused with skepticism. "I thought you didn't recognize the description of the man she'd given you?"

"I didn't. But the man who forced us off the road and shot at us had a tattoo of a snake crawling up the right side of his neck. I saw it when he ran back to the SUV when he heard the police sirens."

Detective Chellel's expression was still skeptical. "So you're thinking it was the same guy?"

Alexis threw up her hands. "How many guys with snake tattoos on their neck do you think are after us?"

"I'm learning not to underestimate you two," Detective Chellel said with more than a hint of derision.

TJ stepped between the two women. "OK, ladies, we're on the same team here." He looked at the detective. "I checked the car for trackers. There were none. I think Mr. Snake followed us from Lenora Kenda's house. He must have gotten spooked when he saw us go into the police station. He's getting desperate. Running us off the road and shooting at us in broad daylight with multiple witnesses was reckless."

Detective Chellel signaled to one of the uniformed officers.

The officer headed their way.

"I'll send a car to Ms. Kenda's house to make sure everything is OK there." Detective Chellel gave the officer his orders before turning back to Alexis and TJ. "You two should go to the hospital to get checked out."

TJ shot a look at Alexis, who shook her head. "We'll be OK. I think the best thing for us right now would be to go home and let me do my job."

"The best thing you can do for me right now, Detective Chellel, is to find the man who attacked us and killed my brother. The best thing you can do for me…" Alexis pressed her hands to her chest and gave the detective an angry glare, "is to do your job."

Detective Chellel sighed. "I know you've just been through a traumatic accident, you're upset and frustrated, but you should know I'm doing everything I can to find out who killed your brother and who is after you now."

"What are you doing standing here, then?" Alexis gestured toward the highway and the traffic that was crawling by. "We gave you a description of the guy and his car. Why aren't you out there looking for him before he tries something like this again? Or worse."

Detective Chellel's expression darkened. "Ms. Douglas, go home. Rest. Stay out of my way." The detective turned on her heel and marched away.

Alexis turned to TJ, her eyes still simmering with anger and frustration. "She wouldn't be anywhere without the information that we got for her. Now she wants us to go home and rest?" Alexis's voice shook with indignation. "With the way she's bungled the investigation so far, we'll never get answers leaving it to her and the police department."

TJ wrapped an arm around Alexis's shoulder. He didn't disagree with Alexis's assessment of the situation, but Detective Chellel wasn't wrong, either. At least not about them both needing to rest. Being driven off the road? Wouldn't leave any lasting damage, but they would soon have new bruises to add to their growing collection of injuries, and he was sure they both would be sore come morning. He also wanted to talk the latest turn of events over with Shawn and make a plan for the next steps. On a scale of dangerousness, they just jumped up several rungs, and TJ was no longer sure it was safe for Alexis to continue to help him with this investigation. But that was a discussion he wanted to have with her when her emotions weren't running so high.

"Detective Chellel is right about us getting some rest. It's getting late, and we both need to recharge and create a plan for the next steps."

For a moment, it looked as if Alexis was going to argue with him, but then her shoulders slumped forward, a sign of resignation.

When she looked up at him again, her eyes were filled with weariness. "You're not giving up on me, are you?"

He met her gaze directly, hoping she would see the resolve in his eyes. "Never. Let's go talk to Jessica Castaldo."

Chapter Twenty

Detective Chellel assigned a patrolman to take them back to the safe house. Alexis knew there was no way TJ was going to allow anyone, not even a police officer, knowledge of the safe house's location, so she wasn't surprised when he asked the cop to drop them off at the nearest rental car location. This car rental company wasn't the same one they'd used at the airport, which was probably for the best since the car they'd rented at the airport was currently being pulled out of a ditch.

Once they were back on the road, TJ called Shawn and gave him a status update. Shawn agreed to take care of the paperwork hassle that was sure to arise out of their being forced off the road and reminded TJ to call if he needed backup.

The address they had for Jessica led them to a newish high-rise apartment building not far from the Potomac River waterfront.

TJ found a parking garage a half block away, and they walked back to the building, stopping for a moment when they reached the entrance and looking up.

"This is definitely a step up from Mark's duplex and her apartment. Jessica is a waitress. How could she afford a place like this?" Alexis asked, looking from the building to TJ.

"Didn't she move in with Mark only a couple of weeks after they started dating?"

Alexis nodded.

"Well, maybe this isn't her place either, but that's definitely one question I want the answer to." TJ reached for the door and held it open to let Alexis enter first.

There was a reception desk, but the doorman must have been occupied elsewhere. They took the opportunity that had been handed to them and walked past the desk quickly. Their luck continued when the elevator doors opened immediately.

They stepped out of the elevator on the tenth floor and headed to Jessica's apartment.

It took several moments before the apartment door was opened, but when it was, Mark's former flame stood before them in colorful leggings and an oversize T-shirt with the collar cut off. The shirt hung off one shoulder, revealing the smooth, tan skin of one of Jessica's shoulders. Surprise darkened her green eyes.

"Alexis, what a nice surprise." The tone of Jessica's voice didn't match the words. She wasn't at all happy to see them on her doorstep.

Alexis flashed a tight smile at her brother's former girlfriend. "Hi, Jessica. Sorry to drop in on you like this, but I wondered if you have a moment to talk?"

Jessica tipped her head to the side, her expression curious. "Sure, I guess." Her eyes swept over TJ appraisingly, lighting a spark of jealousy in Alexis.

"I'm sure you remember TJ," Alexis said. "He's helping me sort out a few details."

Jessica flashed a sultry smile. "I don't mind at all. I remember TJ well." Jessica's smile was openly seductive and only made Alexis dislike her more.

Jessica held the door open for them to enter.

The apartment was open space, almost loft like, and roomy. She had no idea what the place rented for, but it was clear from the condition of the building and the finishes in the apartment that this was not a place a waitress could afford on her own.

Jessica waved them toward a large black leather sectional sofa, taking a seat herself on one end, while he and Alexis sat on the other side.

"So you said you're sorting out some details?" Jessica asked. "I assume about Mark."

"Yes," Alexis answered. "I know Detective Chellel has already spoken to you about Mark. The police believe that he stole from his employer."

Jessica nodded, but her eyes skated away from Alexis's. "I talked to the detective, but I want you to know that I told her that there was no way Mark stole anything."

She may not have liked Jessica, but at least they were on the same page regarding Mark's innocence. "I told Detective Chellel the same thing but, at least until recently, she seems convinced Mark stole the Nimbus program and then killed himself before he could be arrested."

Jessica glanced away. "I don't know anything about that."

Alexis slid a little closer to Jessica. "I think the police are on the wrong track, so I hired TJ. He's not only a friend of Mark's, but he's a private detective. We've been working to clear Mark's name and, well…" Alexis glanced at TJ.

"A little while ago, the detective in charge of the case informed us that Mark's death was going to be ruled a homicide," TJ said. Alexis still couldn't quite bring herself to say it out loud.

A small gasp escaped Jessica's lips, and she pressed a hand to her chest.

It felt overdone to Alexis, as if Jessica was reacting how she thought they expected her to, but not with genuine shock. "Jessica, I need you to tell me the truth. Do you know anything about the theft or what happened to Mark that you didn't tell the cops when they questioned you?"

"What? No, of course not. Why would I? Mark and I had broken up by then." Jessica squared her shoulders, but Alexis read the fear in her eyes before they darted away.

"You're lying," Alexis growled, her patience running thin.

Jessica shifted nervously on the sofa. "You can't just come into my apartment and call me a liar."

"I just did. And speaking of your apartment, how do you pay for this place? It seems way outside the budget for a waitress."

Jessica glared. "It's a sublet. Look, I'm sorry about Mark, but…"

"You're going to be a lot sorrier if you don't tell the truth," Alexis spat.

TJ interrupted. "Jessica, now that the investigation includes a homicide, you can expect the police will be paying you another visit, and I'm sure Detective Chellel is going to ask the same questions in a far less polite manner. It might be best for you if you get out ahead of this. Alexis and I will do what we can to help you."

If Jessica had a hand in Mark's death, the only help Alexis would give her would be getting her to prison, but she knew better than to say that when they needed the woman to tell them whatever she might know.

"You said that you and Mark broke up, but he still had your photo next to his bed."

Jessica shrugged, petulantly. "Okay, so we hooked up a little sometimes. It didn't mean we were headed for marriage."

"Were you hooking up with Mark around the time he was killed?" Alexis asked.

Jessica crossed her arms over her chest and nodded. "Yeah, I guess so."

She still wouldn't meet Alexis's eyes. It was clear there was something she wasn't telling them. Before Alexis could press the point, TJ spoke.

"Jessica." He reached across the sofa and laid his hand lightly on Jessica's leg. "Whatever it is you aren't saying, it will be a lot better to get it out now than to have Detective Chellel drag it out of you."

"I didn't know!" The words burst forth, opening a well of tears. TJ wrapped an arm around Jessica while she cried.

It took a few minutes before she was able to pull herself together and speak again.

"I swear I didn't know anything about a theft or that they were going to hurt Mark."

"I'm sure you didn't," TJ said soothingly.

All Alexis could think was that she was glad he was there, and that he was sitting between her and Jessica. She was more than ready to shake the truth out of the woman if that's what it took, but she marshaled her patience and let TJ take the lead on this part of the questioning, since he seemed to be getting somewhere.

"Tell us what happened so we can help you," TJ coaxed.

"A man came to the diner and asked if I could get Mark's work identification and key fob for him. I… I knew

I shouldn't do it. But he offered me ten thousand dollars. Mark told me he'd help me pay rent on my new place when he broke up with me and I moved out, but he never gave me a dime. I was struggling and so mad at Mark."

Alexis opened her mouth to tell Jessica just how much it had hurt. Her actions had likely been the catalyst for Mark's murder.

TJ spoke before her, though. "Did the man say why he wanted the ID and fob?"

Jessica shook her head. "Not really. He just said he was a friend of Mark's and he was going to play a joke on him."

Alexis couldn't stay quiet any longer. "You can't possibly have believed that."

Jessica turned a tear-filled glare onto Alexis. "I made a mistake. I needed the money." She waved a hand in the air, indicating the apartment.

Ten thousand dollars wasn't a lot when it came to renting a place like this long term, but it would buy a few months of luxury, which was apparently enough for Jessica.

"I convinced Mark we should talk about getting back together. He agreed and invited me to his place. We had a few drinks and then…" Jessica's cheeks reddened. "After he fell asleep I took the ID and fob and texted the guy to come get them. I don't know what he did with them while he had them, but he only had them for like an hour. Two at the most. He slipped them through the mail slot in Mark's door and I put them back before Mark even knew they were missing. I'm sorry, but I didn't have any choice." She sniffled.

"There's always a choice," Alexis spat.

TJ squeezed her thigh. "Can you describe the man who asked you to get Mark's ID for him?" he asked Jessica.

Jessica wiped at her eyes again. "Um…white. Average height, I guess. Dark hair and eyes. There was nothing really special about him. I mean, he wasn't a looker or anything, you know. The only thing that stood out was the tattoo on his neck." She grimaced as if she'd just bitten into something sour. "I usually go for guys with tattoos, but this one, it was so creepy."

"Let me guess," Alexis said, looking from Jessica to TJ. "A coiled snake."

"Yeah." Jessica's eyes opened wide in surprise. "How did you know?"

Chapter Twenty-One

When she and TJ returned to the safe house, Alexis went to her room to shower and change before catching a quick power nap. Despite the renewed sense of hope she felt about clearing Mark's name, she was emotionally and physically exhausted. She only intended to lie down for a few minutes, but she awakened hours later to a darkened room.

She may have needed the sleep, but she wasn't sure how restful it had been. She'd found herself caught in a tantalizingly erotic dream starring TJ that she'd been more than a little disappointed to have awoken from. A dream that had left her libido revved and ready for the real thing.

TJ wasn't the kind of guy who stuck it out for the long term, she knew that. That didn't mean they couldn't enjoy each other's company while they were together. She'd seen the desire in his eyes more than once. She knew he wanted her. And from the way her body was humming at just the thought of taking him into her bed, she couldn't deny she wanted him just as much. She'd never thought of herself as the kind of woman who'd have a fling, but life was about trying new things. And she trusted TJ. More importantly, she wanted him. She was willing to worry about the consequences of that later.

So she was going to try one more time to make him

forget his misguided loyalty or that she was Mark's sister. And if he rejected her a second time? She couldn't think about that now. Not before attempting to seduce TJ Roman.

She crossed the room to the adjoining bathroom and ran a brush through her hair. She'd napped in the oversize T-shirt that hit her mid-thigh and that she normally wore as a pajama top with panties, and nothing else. It wasn't the sexiest outfit, but it would do for an impromptu seduction.

The house was quiet when she patted down the stairs. For a moment, fear sprinted its way through her body until a familiar grunt sounded from beyond the kitchen. She found the garage door open and the lights on. TJ's feet stuck out from under the SUV. He lay on some sort of dolly, and based on the swears coming from underneath the chassis, whatever he was doing wasn't going well.

"Everything okay?" Alexis asked, stopping beside the car next to TJ.

TJ rolled himself out from under the car. His gaze blazed a trail up from her legs to her torso, and finally landed on her face.

The lust she saw in his eyes sent a surge of feminine power through her.

TJ pushed to his feet and cleared his throat. "Everything is fine. I'm just checking the car for trackers or bugs."

Alexis stepped forward, leaving only a sliver of space between them. "In case I haven't said it yet, thank you for helping me." She went onto the tips of her toes and pressed a kiss to his cheek.

She pulled back and watched as TJ swallowed hard, his Adam's apple bobbing.

"Alexis, what are you doing?"

She threaded her arms around his neck. "I think you

know," she whispered in his ear, pressing her breasts against his chest.

A low moan erupted from TJ's throat and his arms came around her waist. "We shouldn't."

She pulled back again, looking into his eyes. "Why not? And don't say Mark. If you don't want me, that's one thing…"

TJ pulled her closer. She felt the hard ridge of his manhood against her thigh.

"You know I do," he growled.

"So take what you want." She feathered kisses along his neck. "What we both want."

TJ didn't move.

For a millisecond, she thought he was going to reject her.

But then he tipped his head, bringing his mouth to hers in a crushing kiss. His mouth was hot and hungry, surpassing everything she'd dreamed and imagined it would be.

She opened to him and he took the kiss deeper, pulling a moan from deep within her. She leaned forward and felt TJ's erection throb between her legs.

Her heart thundered against his chest, its beat becoming wilder and wilder the more he plundered her mouth.

Far too soon, TJ pulled away, his chest rising and falling with rapid breaths. "Are you sure? Really sure?"

She ran her bare foot up his calf. "Absolutely."

TJ took her mouth again, at the same time hoisting her up.

She wrapped her legs around his waist, and she rocked her hips against him.

He let out a low growl that ripped from his throat. "If you keep doing that, I won't be able to go slow."

She rocked again. "Who says I want you to go slow?"

TJ swung them around and walked them into the house.

He lowered her onto the sofa and made quick work of stripping her of her T-shirt and panties. Then she had the pleasure of watching him as he freed himself from his clothes.

He joined her on the sofa, his mouth covering hers again. His hands moved over her body and then he followed with his mouth.

Alexis closed her eyes and let him roam, content, ecstatic even, simply to allow herself to feel. To enjoy the feeling of TJ's mouth on her left breast, and then her right. He kissed his way down her torso to her core and brought her to an explosive climax with his mouth.

Giving her no time to catch her breath, he settled between her legs and plunged deep.

She cried out.

TJ stilled. "Am I hurting you?"

"No. Don't stop," she panted, rolling her hips and pulling him in deeper still.

He shuddered and began moving again with an urgency that had her crying out a second time as he drove her to the edge.

She opened her eyes and watched his jaw tighten as he thrust into her. It was the most erotic sight she'd ever seen, and she rose to meet each thrust, each of them driving the other higher and higher until she broke. Her back arched, and she came harder than she ever had before.

He drove into her one last time with a shudder and moaned her name.

TJ collapsed on top of her, his weight pressing her back into the sofa cushions.

She ran her hand up and down his spine.

"How do you feel?" TJ asked, his head buried in the crook of her neck.

"Pretty damn fine, thank you." She giggled.

TJ lifted his head and looked her in the eye with a wry grin on his lips. "Glad I could be of service."

Chapter Twenty-Two

TJ woke up with Alexis curled into his side. He and Alexis had reached for each other once more during the night for another passionate round of love making. His feelings in tumult, he got out of bed and showered and dressed for the day. Alexis was still asleep when he tiptoed back through the bedroom and into the kitchen, where he got a pot of coffee started and turned once again to the information they'd collected so far on Mark's case. He tried to stop the memories of making love with Alexis from consuming all his thoughts.

"TJ?"

He started at the sound of Alexis's voice.

She wrapped her arms around him from behind and dropped a kiss on his neck that sent a shiver through him. "I called your name twice. What are you reading so intently?"

"Just thinking about our next steps." He raised his head and did a quarter turn in the chair, pulling her into his lap. He captured her lips in a searing good morning kiss that left them both panting for breath by the time they pulled away from each other. They held each other for several moments.

"Good morning," he finally said.

"Good morning." Alexis beamed.

The coffee maker beeped it was ready. Alexis dropped another quick kiss on his lips before pushing to her feet. "I could use a cup. Should I pour you one too?"

"Sure. Thanks."

"I'm planning to whip up omelets for breakfast if that's alright with you?" She grabbed two coffee mugs from an overhead cabinet.

She carried two mugs of coffee to the table and sat across from him. "Umm…should we talk about what happened last night?"

"Last night was amazing," he said, looking directly into her eyes. "But I don't want to give you the wrong idea. I'm still the man who can't give you what you want."

"I don't believe that and I don't believe you do either."

He tore his gaze away from her and looked into his coffee. "Let's just focus on finding answers for Mark now, okay?"

His phone rang, cutting off her answer.

"Roman."

"Mr. Roman, this is Detective Chellel. I have to ask you and Ms. Douglas to come down to the station for some questioning immediately."

The detective's tone wasn't out-and-out hostile, but it wasn't polite either.

"Questioning about what?" TJ pressed.

"It would be better if I explained once you were here."

TJ shot a glance at Alexis, who'd paused her quest for coffee and was watching him intently now.

"Then we're at an impasse. I assume since you're making this call, you can't compel our appearance at the station and neither Alexis nor I are willing to walk into questioning without knowing what this is about and whether we should bring our lawyers with us."

He could almost feel the frustration and annoyance emanating from the detective on the other end of the phone.

"Jessica Castaldo was found deceased in her apartment early this morning. I believe you and Miss Douglas were the last two people to see her alive. Now, will you come in voluntarily, or do I send a patrol car?"

TJ DROVE HIMSELF and Alexis to the police station. They were led to separate interrogation rooms the moment they arrived. He was brought to a bland interview room that smelled vaguely of stale beer and vomit. The uniformed officer who led him to the room offered coffee. TJ declined.

He'd also declined to bring a lawyer with him, although he'd called Shawn on the way to the station. Shawn had cautioned them both not to speak to Detective Chellel without representation and had offered to arrange for an attorney to meet them, but Alexis countered that they had nothing to hide. While he agreed that they didn't have anything to hide, Jessica had been alive and well when they left her apartment. He knew that innocence didn't always carry the day. Still, he figured it couldn't hurt to speak to the detective and get a sense of what had happened after they'd left Jessica's apartment the night before.

But he was getting annoyed at the detective's tactics. He'd been waiting in the interrogation room for more than forty minutes.

Finally, the door opened and Detective Chellel walked in. She slapped a file folder on the table between them and sat, giving TJ a long look. "What were you doing at Jessica Castaldo's apartment yesterday?"

"Alexis and I wanted to find out what she knew about Mark's death."

Chellel scowled. "I told you I'd handle things from here on out. I told you to stay out of my investigation."

TJ leaned back in his chair and folded his hands on his lap. "You have your job, Detective, and I have mine."

"Does your job include murder?"

He couldn't see any benefit in antagonizing the detective. At least, not at the moment.

"It does not and whatever happened to Jessica, neither Alexis nor I had any hand in it."

"You snuck into her building."

"We did no such thing."

Chellel snatched a sheet of paper from the file and slapped it down on the table in front of him. "The building sign-in sheet doesn't have you or Ms. Douglas signing in, and the security tapes show you rushing toward the elevators while the doorman was away from his post."

"I wouldn't call that sneaking in. You said it yourself, the doorman wasn't at his post."

Chellel eyed him with open derision. "Why don't you start from the beginning? What time did you arrive at Ms. Castaldo's apartment?"

He took the detective through the details of his and Alexis's talk with Jessica the night before. The detective let him tell the story the first time through without interruption before asking him to repeat it from the beginning. The second time through, it felt like she stopped him every ten seconds or so to ask a question or drill down on some minute detail. It didn't matter, though. The story wasn't going to change, no matter how many ways she asked the same question.

"So you're saying Jessica admitted to stealing Mark Douglas's employee ID and passing it along to someone who you think then used it to download the Nimbus program?"

"Exactly."

Chellel shook her head. "And I've only got your word about this confession."

"You have Alexis's too. I'm sure she's told you, or she will, the same things I have. We confronted Jessica, and she told us about her role in the theft. And there's your motive for why someone might want her dead."

Chellel's brow arched. "Someone like Alexis Douglas, for instance."

Now TJ shook his head. "No. Alexis doesn't have a motive. She needed Jessica alive and willing to testify to her part in the theft."

"Or," Chellel dragged out the word. "She saw Jessica's actions as having contributed to her brother's death and she sought retribution."

"Or, since we're positing theories here, the man Jessica gave Mark's ID to got spooked and decided to eliminate a potential witness."

"I wonder what could have spooked this hypothetical killer. Maybe you and Ms. Douglas mucking around in my case, perhaps?"

It was a possibility. One he couldn't help feeling a little bit of guilt over. It was entirely possible his and Alexis's visit to Jessica's apartment had led to her death, but the only thing they could do about it now was to help find her killer.

Chellel sifted through the papers in the file. "You're licensed to carry a gun, correct?"

"Correct."

"We'd like to run ballistics on your gun."

"So Jessica was shot?"

Chellel didn't answer.

"You're welcome to run whatever test you'd like. Obviously, I didn't bring a gun into the police station."

"I can have a uniformed officer follow you to wherever you're staying. Which is where?"

TJ smiled. He wasn't about to reveal the location of the safe house. "No need. My sidearm is locked in the glove box."

Chellel frowned. "Then I'll have an officer retrieve it."

TJ didn't love that idea either. No doubt the officer assigned would also be told to snoop around in the car, but he didn't see a way around it. He handed the keys to the rental to the detective.

She rose and left the room for several minutes before returning. "Thank you for being so cooperative. It will take a couple of days for the ballistics guys to do their work. I'll get your weapon back to you as soon as possible."

It annoyed him to be without his favorite gun, but he'd brought several others along for the trip in his go bag. "Not a problem. Can I ask one question, though?"

"You can ask whatever you want. I won't promise to answer."

"Fair enough. What time was Jessica killed?"

Chellel shook her head. "I can't share that information with you."

"Fine." TJ held up his hands. "But if the lobby security recordings show Alexis and I going up to Jessica's apartment, they must show us leaving as well. You know Alexis and I didn't have anything to do with her death."

"I don't know any such thing," the detective said. "There

are security cameras in the lobby, but not at the back door to the building or in the stairwells. You or Ms. Douglas could have been scoping out the building and then come back later in the evening."

"Come on, detective," TJ said incredulously. "We were smart enough to scope out the building but dumb enough to let ourselves get caught on tape the day Jessica was killed? That makes no sense."

Detective Chellel's eyes narrowed into slits. "Murder never makes sense, Mr. Roman. I'll be in touch."

Chapter Twenty-Three

A uniformed officer escorted him as far as the reception area of the police department. Alexis rose from her seat and hurried toward him as soon as he entered.

"Are you alright?" she asked, wrapping her arms around him.

Relief and something else, a feeling as if his world had been righted the moment she stepped into his arms, washed over him.

He pulled her close. "I'm fine. How about you?"

Alexis pulled back enough to look at his face. "Fine. Detective Chellel was a pit bull, but I just told her the truth. We spoke to Jessica. She told us about stealing Mark's ID and fob. We left."

"Same here. Come on, let's get out of here."

They walked to the car, arms still wrapped around each other.

"Where are we going?" Alexis asked once they were inside.

"First, back to the safe house. I need to pick up another weapon. Or two. Detective Chellel took the gun I had in the car for testing."

Alexis shook her head in disgust. "She can't really believe you or I killed Jessica. That's insane."

"I don't think she does," TJ said, steering them in the direction of the safe house. "But she has to do her job."

Alexis frowned but let it go. "You said first to the safe house. Where to second?"

"I thought we'd talk to Lenora Kenda again. I'm convinced there was something she wasn't telling us. If I'm right, she and her daughters could be in real danger."

Alexis looked at him with wide eyes. "You think the guy with the snake tattoo killed Jessica and now he might go after Lenora?"

That's exactly what he thought. "It's as good a theory as any. Killing Jessica strikes me as a cleaning house move. If Lenora is somehow a part of this too, she could be next on this guy's list."

After a quick stop at the safe house where he grabbed his backup weapon, they headed for Lenora Kenda's home.

As TJ turned the car onto Lenora's street, he saw the woman hustling a girl who looked like a younger version of the teenager they'd seen at Lenora's house a day earlier from the front door to the minivan parked in the driveway in front of the house. TJ stopped the car at the corner, a safe distance away, but close enough for him and Alexis to have a good view of Lenora's house.

"What is she doing?" Alexis asked.

"Running," TJ answered.

The younger girl had a pink backpack slung over her shoulder and dragged her purple suitcase on wheels behind her.

"Running from what?"

"That is a very good question. And exactly what we need to know."

If there'd been any doubt in his mind before, Lenora's

current actions would have erased them all. She was hiding something, and TJ could feel that they were running out of time to convince her to tell them what it was.

He and Alexis watched as Lenora threw her daughter's purple suitcase in the trunk and slammed it closed. She shooed her daughter into the backseat and slammed the back door closed before heading for the driver's side door.

Lenora paused, her hand gripping the door handle, and scanned the street. For one brief moment, TJ thought she'd seen them.

Alexis must've thought the same. She slid down a bit in her seat and cast a glance over at him. "Did she see us?"

"I don't think so." He was sure they weren't close enough for Lenora to see them. At least not to see who was inside the car. He may not have extensive experience investigating the big complex cases that West Investigations usually took on, but he knew how to track and follow. It was the bread and butter of his work. Lenora might wonder about the unusual car parked on a street, but she couldn't know they were inside.

After a moment, Lenora opened the door and hopped into the driver's side of the minivan. She backed out of the driveway and headed down the street, away from where they were parked.

TJ shifted the car back into Drive and followed.

Alexis looked at him with a mixture of excitement and curiosity swimming across her face. "We're following her?"

"Unless you have a better idea. We might get more information seeing where she's headed, than we would trying to force her to answer our questions."

Alexis grinned. "You're the expert."

He finally felt like he knew what he was doing, at least when it came to this type of investigation. He knew exactly how far back to stay so that Lenora wouldn't see them, but so that he wouldn't lose her either. He could finally put all the hours he'd spent following cheating husbands and wives to use helping Alexis.

Lenora made a series of turns probably trying to spot if someone was tailing her. He kept following, giving her a long enough tether that he was sure she didn't realize they were behind her.

TJ's cell phone rang.

Alexis peered at the screen. "It's Shawn." She pressed the button to answer the call.

"Shawn, I've got you on speaker. Alexis and I are in the car tailing Lenora Kenda."

"Tailing her? Why?"

"Actually, we just wanted to talk to her, but when we got to her street, we saw her racing from her house to the car with her youngest daughter in tow."

"So what's your plan?"

TJ shot a glance across the car at Alexis. She shrugged her shoulders.

"We don't really have one. It looked kind of suspicious, so we decided to see where Lenora was headed. There's a fifty-fifty chance we're wasting our time. But Lenora is our best lead so far."

"You got good instincts," Shawn said. "I trust them. Think you'll need backup?"

TJ frowned. "You trust my instincts?"

"I do," Shawn said quickly. "But I told you I've got your back, and I meant it. I can hop on a plane and be there in a few hours. You just give the order."

TJ wasn't sure how he felt about Shawn offering to race to his rescue. A bit irritated. A bit relieved to have the offer of backup if he needed it. It had only been a few hours since he noted that the danger factor in this investigation had notched up considerably. And now here he was, going God knows where, and taking Alexis with him. Backup didn't seem like such a terrible idea. But he knew Alexis wouldn't want to wait hours. And neither did he.

"Thanks for the offer but, we don't know where Lenora is going and if we have any chance of getting her to talk to us, it would probably be better if just Alexis and I confronted her. She already knows us."

"Whatever you say," Shawn said. "Just know I'm here for you if you need me. And make sure the GPS on your phone is enabled."

"Copy that." TJ ended the call.

Lenora made a left turn up ahead, and TJ followed several seconds later. Lenora parked the minivan in a driveway belonging to a large redbrick colonial with black shutters and overgrown hedges lining the front of the house. The back door of the minivan opened and Lenora's daughter flew out of the car as the front door of the colonial opened and a man stepped onto the front porch.

The man swept the little girl into his arms and swung her around while Lenora hauled the purple suitcase and the pink backpack from the minivan.

"It looks like she's just dropping her youngest daughter off with her father." Alexis's voice sounded a note of defeat.

"Maybe." TJ wasn't so sure. Everything about Lenora's countenance said she was scared. And if this was just a visitation drop-off, where was her oldest daughter Annie? Something about the situation just felt off.

Lenora made her way up the paved walkway, stopping in front of the man who put the little girl down to take the suitcase and backpack from her.

Lenora and the man spoke briefly before Lenora turned and hurried back to the minivan. The man gave an awkward wave, a curious look on his face, as Lenora peeled out of the driveway and back down the street.

"Where is she going now?" Alexis asked.

"Let's keep following and see." TJ put the car in gear and fell in behind Lenora again.

Chapter Twenty-Four

TJ continued to follow Lenora Kenda at a distance as she drove away from the more populated areas of town and into a decidedly more rural landscape. Alexis was amazed at how far back he could hang without losing her trail.

"Where is she going?" Alexis asked, peering out the windshield at the back of Lenora's minivan.

"I have no idea," TJ responded. "But wherever it is, we can safely say it's off the beaten path."

The wrinkles in TJ's forehead deepened the longer they followed Lenora. Alexis was more than a little worried herself. But she believed they were on the right track following her. Something was definitely up with the woman, and they needed to find out what it was.

The street signs along the side of the road they were on announced they were headed southwest toward the airport. Was Lenora headed out of state? Detective Chellel said that she'd be giving Lenora a heads-up that the man who had threatened Lenora had also run her and TJ off the road the night before. Had the detective's call scared Lenora into running?

Alexis didn't think so. She could definitely see Lenora running, but not without taking her daughters with her.

That meant this trip was about something else. Could

they have been wrong about Lenora not being involved with the theft of the Nimbus program and in Mark's death? Lenora seemed truly broken up by Mark's death, but what did that really mean? She wouldn't be the first murderer to feel remorse for her actions.

Lenora turned off the main highway onto an ill-kept, bumpy asphalt road.

TJ slowed, allowing more distance between their rental car and Lenora's minivan before he too turned onto the road.

"Where is she going?" Alexis muttered just above her breath.

"I don't know." TJ swerved to miss a gigantic pothole in the middle of the desolate street. "But it's going to be hard to tail her without being seen as long as she stays on this road."

Alexis shot a look at him across the car. "We can't lose her." Not after they'd come this far. Not without knowing why she came out here herself.

TJ didn't respond, but the frown lines on his forehead deepened.

The street they were on twisted and turned, heading into an area dense with trees. Alexis's ears popped, indicating that they were also increasing in elevation.

They followed Lenora, seemingly undetected, for another twenty minutes before she made another turn. Moments later they reached the driveway Lenora had turned into, but there was no way they could turn in after her without being noticed.

TJ drove past the driveway's entrance and pulled the car to a stop about a quarter-mile down the road.

Alexis turned in her seat to face him. "Now what?"

TJ reached across her body and opened the glove compartment and pulled out a shiny silver gun she hadn't seen him put inside. "Now you stay in the car and I will see what Lenora is doing here."

Alexis grabbed his arm before he could exit the car. "No way. I told you I wanted to be involved, and I meant every part of this investigation. Where you go I go."

TJ growled in exasperation. "Things have changed. This investigation has gotten increasingly dangerous. I don't want to see you hurt any worse than you already have been, and we don't know what we might be walking into here."

"I understand the potential danger. I'm going to see this through." Alexis gave his arm a reassuring squeeze. "So let's go talk to Lenora."

They got out of the car and Alexis tucked the gun into the waistband of her jeans at her back. Together, she and TJ picked through the overgrowth lining the street back toward the driveway that Lenora had turned into.

"Try to avoid stepping on branches," TJ whispered. "Or making too much noise."

She did the best she could, but it seemed to her that her every footfall thundered through the woods.

Every few steps TJ stopped them and listened to the sound of the birds chirping in the trees above and little critters that Alexis didn't want to think too hard about, scurrying away from the giant humans thundering through their home. Alexis did know what he was looking for, but she could just barely see through the trees to a lake behind the property they were headed for.

Finally, they reached the tree line surrounding what looked to be a ramshackle house in the middle of a clearing. The house had probably, at one point, been a looker. It had certainly been worth something, and probably still was, sitting so close to the lake. Not that the lake seemed to have fared any better than the house. The water was brown and muddy, and Alexis shuddered at the mere thought of swimming in it. Just beyond the waterline was a boathouse, little more than a shack really, and a half-capsized dock. There was no boat in sight.

"What now?" Alexis repeated the same question she posed in the car.

She turned to look at TJ, but he was frozen, perked, as if he was listening for something coming their way. A palpable fear raced through the woods and surrounded her.

TJ whirled, but he was a fraction of a second too late.

Alexis saw the baseball bat, heard the terrifying crunch as it met the side of TJ's head, and watched the man she cared about more than she was ready to admit, even to herself, crumple to the grass.

She processed it all a split second before the man turned toward her, swinging the bat again.

She had just enough time to register the man's sinister glower and the oiled snake on his neck before the bat connected with the side of her skull with a dull thud that reverberated through her body a millisecond before everything went black.

Chapter Twenty-Five

The pain was excruciating. For the first several moments while he regained consciousness, it was all he could think about. His head felt like it had been cracked into a dozen pieces with the sharp edges stabbing into his brain. But pain meant that he was still alive, although that felt like a slim silver lining at the moment.

"TJ? TJ, can you hear me? TJ, you need to wake up."

Alexis's soft voice cut through the pain reverberating through his head.

"TJ, we're going to need your help if we're going to get out of here. Come on, wake up. Wake up, please."

It was a struggle, but TJ finally forced his eyes to open. Thankfully, wherever they were was shrouded in almost complete darkness. The only light emanated from a single bulb hanging from a chain in the ceiling. He was lying on the hard wooden planks of a floor on his side, his hands bound behind his back.

A sudden awareness jolted through him that they were in deep trouble, followed by a terror he hadn't felt since his time deployed in the military. "Alexis?" His voice came out a croak.

"I'm okay." Her voice came from somewhere behind

his head. "But Lenora Kenda is here with us. And so is her daughter Annie."

TJ struggled to sit up. A wave of pain surged through his brain, forcing him to bite back a cry. He finally got himself into a sitting position, his back resting against what felt like a wooden post, and took stock of his current situation.

He remembered hearing a sound behind him and Alexis as they crept up on the house they'd seen Lenora Kenda enter. He remembered a searing pain and then nothing.

It was obvious that someone had gotten the jump on them. He turned his head slowly in the direction Alexis's voice had come from.

Alexis sat with her legs stretched out in front of her against the wall parallel to the post he was leaning against. Lenora Kenda and her daughter Annie sat next to Alexis. All three had their hands tied in front of them instead of behind them, as his were. Alexis was the only one of the three women who wore an angry red gash just below her hairline and above her ear.

Rage swam through him. Forgetting for a moment that his hands were tied behind his back, he tried moving closer. A fresh surge of pain ricocheting through his head knocked him back.

"Sit still," Alexis ordered. "He hit you pretty hard, and you've been out for a while."

TJ's head still throbbed with pain, but Alexis was right. They had to get out of here, and it would be easier to do that if his hands weren't tied behind his back. He scanned the room for a weapon or anything else that could be useful. There wasn't much. It appeared they'd been brought to the ramshackle boathouse he'd seen as he and Alexis were making their way through the woods toward the house.

From where he was sitting it looked like a good stiff wind could blow the boathouse over, and it was clear that it hadn't been used in any number of years. A threadbare blanket with holes that made it look like an animal had mistaken it for a possible snack lay alone in a corner. A single oar hung forlornly on the wall. Neither would be any help to him.

He flexed his wrists, testing the ropes that bound his hands. They were tight, but not overly so. He started working on getting his hands free, flexing and unflexing his wrists while simultaneously rubbing the rope against the wooden post at his back. Hopefully, the combination of tension would break the twine, or at least loosen it enough for him to slip his hands free.

TJ groaned. "Who? Who hit me?"

"Brock Chavez," Lenora said.

TJ shifted his gaze to Lenora. "All this time you knew who was behind all this, didn't you?"

Annie leaned against her mother, her hands in her mother's lap. Lenora grasped her daughter's tied hands and looked down, but not before TJ saw the guilt swimming in her eyes.

Lenora nodded. "The man I told you about in Mark's office that night... I recognized him. I'd seen him around the office before. Not often, but always in the executive suite."

"So he works for TalCon," Alexis said, disgust in her voice.

Lenora shook her head. "No. Not for TalCon. For Nelson Bacon."

"And you said nothing," Alexis spat, the disgust in her voice now tinged with rage.

"I had to protect my daughters," Lenora shot back. "The

threats I told you about were real. I was afraid. And with good reason. He kidnapped my Annie."

TJ's head was clearing quickly, but something about what Lenora was telling them didn't make sense. "You hadn't given up Chavez or Bacon, so why kidnap your daughter?"

"They knew I talked to you." Lenora's angry glare darted from TJ to Alexis and back. "I got a phone call after you left my house yesterday."

Lenora's words confirmed it. Brock Chavez must have been the man who had followed him and Alexis from Lenora's house to the police station before forcing them off the road.

"I planned to pack up the girls and take them to my sister's house in Florida after they got home from school today. But then I got another call." Tears slid from Lenora's eyes. She huddled closer to her daughter. "He had Annie."

"Why didn't you call the police?" Alexis asked, her tone marginally softer than it'd been moments earlier.

"He told me not to. He said he would kill Annie if he even suspected I called the police. I couldn't take a chance. He told me to drive out to this address." Lenora glanced between them again, desperation in her gaze. "I knew it was a trap, but what choice did I have? I dropped my youngest daughter off with her father, and I did what he told me to do. How did you find me?"

"We were coming to talk to you again. We saw you speeding away from your house." TJ continued to work the rope binding his hands. It was loosening, but not fast enough. "It looked suspicious, so we decided to follow."

Lenora glared. "Now your nosiness is going to get us all killed."

Alexis guffawed. "You can't be serious? Chavez and Bacon were going to kill you no matter what."

The sound of footsteps outside forestalled any response Lenora might have made.

TJ looked at Alexis. "The gun?"

Alexis shook her head. "It was gone when I came to, along with my cell phone."

TJ felt the absence of the familiar weight he usually wore around his ankle. Chavez had taken his gun and cell phone as well.

He worked the ropes against the jagged edges of the pole faster and said a silent prayer.

The rope snapped just as the door to the boathouse opened and the man who had driven them off the road stepped through, holding a gun in his hand.

"I see you all have finally awoken. That's great. It'll be easier to dispose of you."

Chapter Twenty-Six

Alexis wasn't sure she'd ever hated a person as much as she hated the man who hovered over them now, holding a gun. The thought had barely run its course through her head before Nelson Bacon stepped into the boathouse and stopped next to Chavez.

"You killed Mark," Alexis spat. It was all she could do to fight back the urge to lunge at Nelson and wrap her hands around his throat.

A sad expression fell over Bacon's face. "Actually, that was my associate here." Bacon placed a hand on Chavez's shoulder, but quickly removed it when Chavez shot a glare at him. "I am truly sorry about Mark, but I was left with no other choice."

"And what exactly are you up to?" TJ asked.

"Well, I plan to sell Nimbus to the highest bidder, of course," Bacon responded, as if his plans should've been obvious to all.

"But it doesn't even work," Alexis spat.

Bacon waved a hand, unconcerned. "My bidders don't know that and by the time they figure it out, I'll be long gone with their money."

"Mark found out and he was going to stop you, wasn't he?" Alexis said.

Bacon sighed. "He overheard a conversation he shouldn't have. I tried to reason with him. I even offered him a cut. But he couldn't be reasoned with."

"You mean you tried to blackmail him and he wouldn't be blackmailed?" TJ said, feeling a swell of pride for his late friend.

"Why would you do this?" Alexis growled. "You're the CEO of a major military contracting company. You make millions of dollars a year. What more could you want?"

"There's always more to want," Bacon growled. "Especially when the company you've devoted your life to is about to put you out to pasture."

Anger and disgust swelled in Alexis's chest. "So that's it? All this… Mark and Jessica's murders, the attempts on TJ and me, kidnapping, and now what, four more murders? All because you're mad you're being forced to retire with a several million dollar parachute, I'm sure?"

"It sounds terrible when you say it like that." Bacon gave a little shrug. "But it's a matter of loyalty. I've been loyal to TalCon for over twenty years, and now just when the company is about to embark on a new phase in the design of weapons that will send their profits into the stratosphere, they want to cut me out," Bacon barked. "I won't stand for it!"

"Enough chitchat," Chavez said. He handed the weapon in his hand to Bacon and stepped toward TJ. "Keep the gun on them."

As Chavez reached down to haul TJ to his feet, TJ lashed out with a punch that caught Chavez in the nose. Blood gushed.

TJ lashed out with another vicious punch.

Bacon stood frozen, seemingly unsure of what to do about the rapid turn of events.

Alexis didn't waste a moment. She scrambled to her feet and launched herself at Bacon. She threw her shoulder into his gut and heard the air whoosh from his lungs.

Her hands were still tied together, but she was able to use them to gain purchase by balancing herself against Bacon's shoulders before driving her knee into his torso.

The gun fell from Bacon's hand and clattered to the floor.

Alexis followed where it landed, but Bacon was too fast for her. He grabbed her around the ankle and took her to the floor, pulling her back toward him before she could reach the gun. She flipped over onto her back and with the leg Bacon wasn't holding onto, kicked out, catching him in his jaw.

Bacon swore loudly. "I'm going to make you pay for that."

Bacon lunged for her just as a primal scream reverberated around the small boathouse. "Nobody moves!" Lenora stood, her feet shoulder width apart, the gun held out in front of her, her still-tied hands shaking.

Everyone in the room did as Lenora ordered and froze.

"Annie," Lenora said, her voice shaking almost as much as her hands, "get out of here. Go on. Run, find help."

Tears streamed down the teenager's face. She'd crawled into a corner of the boathouse and curled herself into a ball, tucking her head into her knees. She looked up now at her mother. "I don't want to leave you, Mom."

Lenora sent a soft smile in her daughter's direction. "It's okay. I'll be okay. But I need to know that you're safe. Go now."

Annie hesitated for a moment longer before getting to

her feet and heading for the boathouse door. There she paused again, looking at her mother.

Lenora nodded her encouragement. "Hurry."

Annie took off and Lenora turned back toward the adults who were still in the boathouse.

Bacon rose slowly, his hands in the air. "This doesn't have to get ugly, Ms. Kenda. I can make it worth your while if you just let me leave here."

Lenora shot Bacon a venomous look. "You terrorized me. You kidnapped my daughter. You had this thug…" The gun swung in Chavez's direction.

Chavez stuck his hands in the air, the first real signs of fear dancing across his face.

TJ took a step back, away from Chavez. "Lenora, you don't want to do this. Bacon and Chavez will pay. Just hand me the gun."

The sound of sirens pierced the air.

Lenora turned toward the sound.

Seeing his chance, Bacon sprung to his feet and ran for the door of the boathouse.

Chavez also seized the moment. He lunged toward Lenora.

TJ grabbed him before he could reach Lenora and landed a punch to his jaw. Chavez fell to the boathouse floor, out cold.

Alexis eased to Lenora's side. "Come on, Lenora. Let me have the gun." She reached for the gun with a slow, deliberate motion.

Lenora appeared to be in a state of shock. She didn't put up any resistance as Alexis eased the gun from her hand.

The sirens were almost on top of them now.

TJ hobbled to Alexis's side and took the gun. He flung

it out of the boathouse door and toward the surrounding trees. "We should go out with our hands up so they know we're not a threat."

Lenora started for the boathouse door with her hands held high above her head.

"What about Bacon?" Alexis said.

TJ pulled her to him and pressed a kiss to her hairline. "He couldn't have gotten far. We'll let the authorities know to be on the lookout for him."

Alexis met his gaze. "I did it. The men who killed my brother are going to have to answer for it."

TJ smiled at her. "You did it, baby. You did it."

Chapter Twenty-Seven

TJ sat next to Alexis's hospital bed and watched her sleep, committing every inch of her face to memory. The doctors had given them both a thorough checkup, and despite nasty bumps on the head, neither had a concussion. Alexis's hands had been bound by zip ties, which had cut into the skin around her wrists and that had required some tending to. She'd gotten lucky and hadn't aggravated any of her prior injuries. The nurse tasked with gathering Alexis's discharge papers had gotten pulled into an emergency. Alexis had fallen asleep waiting for her to return.

TJ was dreading the nurse's return. It meant he would have no more excuses for not doing what he knew he had to do. Walk away for good.

The case was over. Annie and Lenora Kenda had been checked out at the hospital. Annie was rattled but unhurt. He and Alexis had given their statements to Detective Chellel at the scene before being transported to the hospital. It certainly wouldn't be the last time they talked to the cops, but it was all a formality now. Nelson Bacon had been caught speeding down the highway in an attempt to get away from the scene. He wasn't talking, but Chavez was singing like a canary.

An experienced criminal with a rap sheet as long as a

book, Chavez knew how it worked. The first to talk got the best deal. Chavez didn't have the smarts or know-how to pull off the theft of the Nimbus program on his own. Bacon was the mastermind behind the plan to steal Nimbus, according to Chavez, which had initially amounted to stealing the program, selling it to the highest bidder and setting up Mark as the fall guy. Bacon didn't have the stomach for the violence, but Brock Chavez had already done time for manslaughter and he had no problem with it. Surprisingly, it appeared that Arnold Forrick hadn't known anything about what Bacon and Chavez were up to.

Chavez copped to kidnapping Annie Kenda, killing Jessica, firebombing Mark's apartment and breaking into Alexis's house in a bid to stop her from investigating Mark's death. He'd also admitted to driving TJ and Alexis off the road and to getting a couple of friends to attack them at the hotel in Alexandria. He'd also administered the overdose of fentanyl to Mark. Detective Chellel cautioned that there was a lot of work still to be done, but it was clear that Mark was nothing more than an innocent victim.

Alexis's eyes fluttered open. She smiled when she caught sight of TJ sitting next to her bed. "Hey, you."

"Hey, how are you feeling?"

"Better now that I've had a little sleep," she said, sliding into a sitting position on the bed. She reached out a hand, but he avoided taking it.

Alexis frowned. "What's wrong?"

A sharp pain pierced TJ's chest at the thought of what he was about to do. He pushed to his feet. "I should go see what's keeping the nurse with the discharge papers."

Alexis sat up straighter and frowned. "No, you should tell me what's wrong. TJ?"

"Bacon and his lackey are in jail. We've proved that Mark didn't kill himself and wasn't a thief. You're safe now. The case is over. And I think it's best if we both went back to our real lives."

"You think it's best, huh?" Alexis pressed the back of her hand to her forehead and TJ's heart gave a jolt at the sight of the white bandages coiled around her wrists.

"I'm not the type of man who can go the distance," he said, his voice barely above a whisper. Guilt and shame engulfed him, but he knew what he was saying was true. He wasn't the man Alexis needed. The kind she deserved.

Alexis glared at him with a mixture of hurt, anger and disappointment. "So that's it? I don't even get a say?"

"I don't think there's anything to say. We both know this can't be anything more than what it was."

"No, we both don't," she responded fiercely. "I'm sorry that you lost Lyssa, but you're just scared now. I'm asking you to take a risk. With me. Together."

TJ felt as if his chest were being pried open. "I can't. I'm sorry. I'm just not the right man for you."

Alexis stared at him for a moment longer before turning away. "If that's what you believe, then go."

TJ hesitated for a moment, his feet feeling as if they were rooted to the spot. He knew this was one of those moments. A defining moment. One that would change the trajectory of his life.

The door to the room suddenly opened, and Alexis's missing nurse hustled into the room.

"So sorry for the delay," the nurse said breathlessly. She thrust a tablet at Alexis and proceeded to explain how the doctor wanted her to take care of her injuries and where Alexis needed to sign before she could leave.

TJ turned and headed for the door.

"TJ."

The sound of Alexis's voice stopped him before he stepped through the door. He turned back to face her.

Alexis sat up straight, her eyes trained just beyond his shoulders. "Thank you for everything."

His eyes stung. "If you ever need anything, anything at all, call. I'll be there."

Her gaze finally met his. "Goodbye, TJ."

"Goodbye, Alexis."

Chapter Twenty-Eight

Alexis pulled open the heavy entrance door to the upscale soul food restaurant. Her restaurant soon if Kitty's offer was still good. She'd decided to take the leap and invest with her friend. The space was coming along. Tables and chairs set out in no particular order yet littered the dining space. The walls had been painted a creamy beige color and the rich wood trim lining the tops and bottoms of the walls had been stained and glossed to a high shine. The dark mahogany bar was in place at the back of the restaurant space, and two workmen were currently installing the shelves that would hold an assortment of liquors for the patrons.

Her and Kitty's dream restaurant come to life.

If she had learned anything over the last couple of weeks, it was not to take anything in life for granted. Some risks were worth taking even if they didn't work out in the end.

Her thoughts turned to TJ. Falling in love with him had been a risk, and she'd known that from the beginning. It'd been over a month since he walked out of her hospital room and she hadn't heard from him since she'd flown home. Alone.

She didn't expect to hear from him either. But she didn't regret falling in love with him. She couldn't. He'd been a risk worth taking, even though her heart was now shattered into a million little pieces.

Kitty pushed her way out of the kitchen carrying a tray of glasses. A smile bloomed on her face when she saw Alexis standing in the middle of the space.

"Yay! You're finally here." Kitty set the glasses on a nearby table and wrapped Alexis in a hug. "I've been dying for you to see the space. It's come a long way, and we're almost ready to hold a soft open."

"It looks fabulous," Alexis said, stepping out of Kitty's embrace and doing a slow spin to take in as much of the space as she could. Kitty had done a great job. The space was almost exactly as Alexis had imagined it from all of their brainstorming sessions in school and after.

She turned back to face her best friend. "You've done an amazing job, Kitty. I'm sorry I wasn't more help."

Kitty threw her arm around Alexis's shoulder and gave it a squeeze. "What are you talking about? You've been there through all of this. Supporting me. Giving me advice. Listening to me moan and groan. The perfect best friend."

Alexis cleared her throat, her heart pounding. "I'm glad to hear you say that. And I'm hoping that your offer to take me on as a partner is still good."

Kitty squealed. "Good? Of course it's still good! The dream wouldn't be complete without you, and I never doubted you'd come to your senses." Kitty engulfed her in another hug.

Alexis laughed. "Well, I'm glad one of us never doubted it."

Kitty shuffled Alexis over to a table and both of them took a seat. They spent the next hour hashing through the terms of the partnership. Alexis would take over executive chef duties at the new restaurant while Kitty continued to run the food truck and operations in the older space. Kitty had applied for a line of credit on her house in order to cover the remaining expenses of the new restaurant. But now, with Alexis's investment, she would not need to take that extraordinary step.

"I'll have my attorney draw up paperwork outlining everything we've just said ASAP," Kitty said.

"That's great." Alexis grinned.

"Now," Kitty said, her tone sobering, "let's talk about TJ."

Alexis felt the smile fall from her face. "There's nothing to talk about."

Kitty cocked her head to the side. "So you haven't spoken to him since the hospital?"

"No. And I don't plan to. He made it very clear he didn't want to be with me. I'm not going to beg."

Kitty reached across the table and took Alexis's hands in hers. "I'm not suggesting that you do, but I can't help but notice that you've been moping around for the last month. If he's half as miserable as you've been, maybe there's a chance you two can work this out."

"He hasn't called." Alexis felt tears welling behind her eyes. "If he felt anything like I feel, he would've called, right?"

Kitty gave Alexis's hands a squeeze and looked at her with sympathy in her eyes. "Oh honey, men aren't that smart."

Alexis chuckled, knowing her friend was trying to lighten the mood even though her heart still felt as if it had been lined in lead.

"I just hate to see you so unhappy," Kitty said.

One of the workmen called Kitty over. Kitty gave

Alexis's hands one more squeeze before she stood and headed for the workmen.

Kitty was right. Alexis had been moping around for a month. Hoping that TJ would call, apologize, and they'd somehow find a way back to each other. But it was time for that to end. She was embarking on a new adventure now, and TJ Roman wasn't a part of it.

TJ WATCHED THE clock on his dashboard tick over from 8:59 to 9:00. He followed the cheating husband West Investigations had been hired to follow as part of the multimillion-dollar divorce between the CEO of one of the biggest conglomerates in the country and his wife. He'd gotten a dozen photographs of the CEO entering the motel, across from which he now sat, with a young, buxom blonde. That had been more than an hour ago and neither of them had come out of the motel room yet.

He'd taken a couple weeks off of work after wrapping up Alexis's case. When he returned, Shawn had offered to put him on one of the more complex cases. Shawn hadn't pulled any punches, stating outright that TJ was wasting his skills, talents and experience photographing cheats and liars. He knew Shawn was right, but ever since he walked out of Alexis's hospital room, he'd had trouble mustering the will to care about much of anything.

He almost called her more than a dozen times, but each time he stopped himself before the call connected. He wanted to be with Alexis more than he wanted air to breathe, but he made a promise.

Someone knocked on the passenger side window, startling TJ from his thoughts.

"Open up," Shawn said.

TJ unlocked the doors, and Shawn slid inside the car.

"You scared the dickens out of me," TJ said grumpily.

"Because you were daydreaming. Or should I say brooding?" Shawn shot him a knowing look.

"I wasn't brooding."

"You've been brooding for the last month and a half. And to be honest it is getting old. Why don't you just call Alexis, tell her what a fool you've been, and beg her to take you back?"

TJ shot a glance at his friend. "There is no back. We were never together."

Shawn guffawed. "You really are a fool if you believe that. You're in love with her. And she's in love with you. I don't understand what the problem is?"

"The problem is, I don't do relationships, and she does. The problem is, she deserves someone better than me. The problem is, I made a promise to a friend and I don't plan to break that promise."

"Look, man, I understand. In general, it's a sound rule to keep your hands off your best friend's sister. But Mark is gone and I doubt he would want to see you in the state you're in over Alexis. I bet if he knew how much you cared for his sister, he'd be ecstatic because I'm sure more than anything what he would have wanted is for his sister and his best friend to be happy."

TJ's heart clenched and unclenched. He and Shawn sat in silence for several long moments before he spoke again. "It's not just the promise. I'm not sure I can go through it all again. Losing Lyssa felt like someone had ripped my heart out."

Shawn sighed. "Losing someone we love, man, is hard for everyone. I can't imagine what it felt like to lose Lyssa.

But I think you have to ask yourself, is living right now, without Alexis, the woman you're in love with today, any better?"

The question lingered in the car, but TJ knew the answer. It was worse.

Yes, he made a promise to Mark. But when Mark had extracted that promise, he'd done so out of love for Alexis and out of a desire to protect her. Mark couldn't do that anymore, but TJ could, and dammit, he wanted to. When Lyssa was taken from him, there was nothing he could do about that. It was fate. But losing Alexis, that was all on him.

TJ groaned.

Shawn smiled. "Glad to see you're on the road to figuring it out. Now, what do you plan to do about fixing the mess you've made?"

"I have no idea. I can't just call Alexis now. I don't even know if she would take my call. I couldn't blame her if she didn't."

Shawn grinned. "I've got an idea, but there's no guarantee it'll work, and I will need help."

The sparkle in Shawn's eyes sent a shot of hope surging through TJ. "Let's hear it. I'm ready to do whatever it takes to win Alexis back."

ALEXIS LET OUT a deep breath and marveled at the crowd of people that filled the restaurant. It was their "soft opening" where they invited all of their investors, close friends, and industry influencers in order to wine and dine them into generating a buzz. So far, the night had progressed well. Everyone seemed to be enjoying themselves, the booze and, most importantly, the food. She'd gotten dozens of compliments about the menu that left her feeling triumphant.

It was a much-needed confidence boost since she wasn't used to having so many people eat her food. Kitty had even insisted she lose her usual armor, otherwise known as her chef's coat, and don a cocktail dress for the event. Alexis had to admit, the dress Kitty had picked out for her made her body look amazing. Sleeveless black lace with a plunging neckline and a pair of Kitty's strapless silver heels had her feeling like a supermodel. And it was clear the men in attendance had noticed. She'd received more than one appreciative glance and had had more men flirt with her in the last couple of hours than had flirted with her in the last year. Still, for some reason, all the male attention had made her melancholy.

There was only one man's attentions she wanted, and he wasn't even there.

Her breath hitched in her chest as she pushed back an impending sob.

Almost as if she'd been summoned, Kitty appeared at Alexis's shoulder. "Smile," she hissed. "It's a party. Happy, happy."

"I am happy." Alexis stretched her mouth into a smile and tried to get into the party spirit. "See."

"Girl, you look like one of those creepy heritage dolls my grandmother used to collect," Kitty said, grimacing. "Why don't you take a moment? Pull yourself together and remember this here is your dream come true. We could use a couple more bottles of champagne. Can you grab a few? There's an open case in the party room."

Alexis accepted the offer of a reprieve, heading down the short hall that led toward the room she and Kitty had dubbed "the party room." They planned to use the room to host larger private parties once they got the restaurant up off the ground, but for now it was being used as a storeroom.

At least that's what it had been used for the last time Alexis had been in it. This time when she stepped into the room, she found that someone had cleared everything out of it except a small table that had been set with a white tablecloth, place settings, roses and candles. The lights were turned down low and twinkling fairy lights hung from the ceiling.

Alexis stepped into the room, confused but curious.

"Kitty said you wouldn't mind being pulled away from the festivities."

She turned toward the door leading from the kitchen into the private room.

TJ stood there in a black tailored suit and an electric blue tie. In his hands was a single red rose.

Alexis just stared for a moment. It was almost as if he were an apparition. It didn't make any sense for him to be there, and yet there he was, looking so much more handsome than she remembered.

Her chest tightened, and her heart pounded furiously. "What are you doing here?"

"I…" The word came out as a croak, and TJ cleared his throat before starting again. "I wanted to see you."

Her heart raced. "Why?"

"To apologize. I'm an idiot."

Alexis felt a small smile tip the ends of her mouth upward. "Great start so far."

TJ took several steps toward her, closing the space between them. "I'm so sorry I walked out on you that day in the hospital. I let my fear of losing you, like I lost Lyssa, overshadow the fact that I love you more than anything else in this world."

Alexis thought her heart might just fly right out of her chest.

"You do?"

TJ moved closer. There were only a few inches between them now. "I do. If you give me the chance, I'll make sure you know it every single day for the rest of your life."

Tears sprang into Alexis's eyes. "Are you sure? I mean, you made a promise to Mark and your feelings about relationships..."

TJ reached out and took her hands into his. "It took me a while, but I finally realized those are just excuses. I was scared. Of losing you. So scared that I pushed you away and risked losing you anyway."

Alexis chuckled. "Yeah, that didn't make much sense, did it?"

TJ gave her a smile. "No, it didn't. I needed a little help to see that, but I see it now. I just hope it's not too late." He looked at her with a question in his eyes.

Alexis bit her bottom lip, but it did nothing to stop the tears rolling down her cheeks. "It's not too late." She stepped into TJ's embrace, wrapping her arms around his waist. "It would've never been too late. My heart belongs to you, and it always will."

TJ let out a shuddering breath that shook them both. "I love you, Alexis, and I promise I will never leave your side again."

When he captured her mouth with his a second later, she knew she could count on that promise forever.

* * * * *

Look for more books in K.D. Richards's
West Investigations series,
when Lakeside Secrets
comes out next month!

   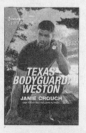